4155

Cemetery World

BY THE SAME AUTHOR

Clifford D. Simak

Cemetery World

G. P. PUTNAM'S SONS
New York

FIRST PUBLISHED IN ANALOG

SBN: 399-11071-2
Library of Congress Catalog
Card Number: 72-83333

C. 2

Cemetery World

1

The Cemetery stretched away in the morning light, a thing of breathless beauty. The rows of gleaming monuments swept across the valley and covered all the slopes and hills. The grass, mowed and clipped with precise devotion, was an emerald blanket that gave no hint of the rawness of the soil into which it thrust its roots. The stately pines, planted in the aisles that ran between the rows of graves, made soft and moaning music.

"It gets you," said the captain of the funeral ship.

He thumped his chest to show me exactly where it got him. He was an oaf, this captain.

"You remember Mother Earth," he told me, "all the days you're gone, all the years in space and on the other planets. You call up in your mind exactly what it's like. Then you land and open up the port and walk out on its surface and it hits you, suddenly, that you've remembered only half of it, Mother Earth is too big and beautiful to hold it all in mind."

Behind us, on its pad, the funeral ship still sizzled with the heat it had picked up in making planetfall. But the crew was not waiting for the heat to dissipate. Far up its black sides ports were swinging open and cranes were cranking out, with the clank and clatter of the running chains, for the unloading of the cargo. From a long, low building which I took to be a staging shed, vehicles were scuttling across the field to receive the caskets.

The captain paid no attention to what was going on. He

stood staring at the Cemetery. He seemed fascinated with it. He made an all-inclusive gesture at it.

"Miles and miles of it," he said. "Not only here in North America, but in other places. This is just a corner of it."

He wasn't telling me anything that I didn't know. I had read all there was to read of Earth. I had viewed and listened to every scrap of tape bearing on the planet that I could lay my hands upon. I had dreamed of Earth for years and studied it for years and finally was here and this great clown of a captain was making a silly sideshow of it. As if he, personally, might own it. Although that, perhaps, was understandable, for he was Cemetery.

He was right, of course, about this being but one small corner of it. The monuments and the velvet carpeting of grass and that stately marching of the pines swept on for miles and miles. Here in ancient North America and in the olden isle of Britain and the continent of Europe, in northern Africa and China.

"And every foot of it," the captain said, "as well-kept and tended, as beautiful and peaceful, and as solemn as this small corner of it."

"And what about the rest of it?" I asked.

The captain swung angrily toward me. "The rest of it?" he asked.

"The rest of Earth. It's not all Cemetery."

"It seems to me," the captain said, somewhat sharply, "that you've asked that before. You seem obsessed with it. The thing to understand is that the Cemetery is the only part of it that counts."

And that was it, of course. In all the recent literature of Earth—recent being the last thousand years or so—there was seldom any mention, anywhere, of the rest of Earth. The Earth was Cemetery, if one excepted those few places of historic or cultural interest that were so highly advertised and promoted by the Pilgrim Tours, and even in the case of the Pilgrim attractions one gained the impression that they were set aside and preserved for future generations by Cemetery generosity. Aside from that, there was no mention, or only fleeting mention, of any other Earth—as if all the rest of Earth were no more than ground waiting to become a part of Cemetery, as if it were no more than lonely, empty terrain so long untenanted that even the memories of ancient times had long since been erased.

The captain continued to be severe with me. "We shall unload your freight," he told me, "and store it in the shed. Where you can reach it easily. I'll ask the men to be sure not to mix it with the caskets."

"That is kind of you," I said. I was disenchanted with this captain. I had seen too much of him—on the third day out I'd seen too much of him. I had done my best to keep away from him, but that is hard to do when you're aboard a funeral ship and are technically the captain's guest—although I had paid rather handsomely to become his guest.

"I hope," he said, still speaking in a slightly outraged tone, "that your freight does not contain anything of seditious nature."

"I was not aware," I told him, "that the status of Mother Earth, Inc., was such as to allow sedition."

"I did not ask you," he said, "I did not inquire too closely. I had taken you to be a man of honor."

"Honor did not enter into our arrangement," I said. "It was of a purely monetary nature."

Perhaps, I told myself, I should not have made any mention of the rest of Earth. We had talked of it before, of course, and I could see, even from the first, that it was a very touchy subject. I could have suspected that much from all that I had read and I should have kept my mouth shut. But it was a thing that was very close to me, the conviction that Old Earth, even in ten thousand years, could not have become an entirely faceless planet. One who went to look, I was convinced, still would find old scars, old triumphs, ancient memories written in the dust and stone.

The captain had turned to walk away, but I asked another question. "This man," I said. "The manager. The one I am to see."

"His name," said the captain, stiffly, "is Maxwell Peter

Bell. You'll find him over there, in the administration building."

He pointed toward the gleaming massiveness of a great white building at the far end of the field. A road ran out to reach it. It would be a fairly long hike, but I would enjoy walking, I told myself. There was no means of transportation in sight. All the cars that had come out from the staging shed were lined up waiting for the caskets from the ship.

"That other building over there," the captain said, pointing once again, "is the hotel operated by the Pilgrim Tours. You probably will be able to find accommodations there."

Then, having done his duty for me, the captain went stalking off.

The hotel, a ground-hugging structure not more than three stories high, was a great deal farther off than the administration building. Other than the two buildings and the ship standing on the pad, the entire place was empty. There were no other ships upon the field and, other than the cars waiting by the ships, no traffic.

I started for the building. It would be pleasant, I thought, to stretch my legs, good to feel solid ground underneath my feet, good to breathe pure air again after months in space. And good to be on Earth. There had been many times I had despaired of ever getting there.

Elmer, more than likely, would have his nose all out of joint at my failing to uncrate him as soon as we made planetfall. It would have made good sense to do so, for if he were uncrated he could be setting up the Bronco while I was seeing Bell. But I would have had to wait around until the crates had been unloaded and taken to the shed and I was anxious to be doing something, anxious to get started.

I wondered, as I walked along, just why I should be calling on this Maxwell Peter Bell. A courtesy call, the captain had told me, but that didn't quite hold water. There had been damn little courtesy connected with this trip; there had, rather, been hard cash, the last of Elmer's lifelong savings. It was, I thought, as if Cemetery were some sort of government, entitled to diplomatic courtesy from everyone who might come visiting. But it was no such thing at all. It was a simple business, coldly cynical in nature. For a long, long time, in my study of Old Earth, my regard for Mother Earth, Inc., had been very, very low.

2

Maxwell Peter Bell, manager of Mother Earth, Inc.,
North American division, was a pudgy man who wanted to
be liked. He sat in his worn, stodgy, well-upholstered chair
behind the heavy, shining desk in the penthouse office atop
the administration building. He rubbed his hands together
and smiled almost tenderly at me, and I would not have
been surprised if the round, soft brownness of his eyes had
begun to melt and run down his cheeks, leaving chocolate
stains.

"You had a pleasant trip?" he asked. "Captain An-
derson made you comfortable?"

I nodded. "As comfortable as possible. I am grateful, of
course. I did not have the money to buy passage on a
Pilgrim ship."

"You must not think of gratitude," he insisted gently. "It
is we who should be glad. There are few persons of the arts
who evince an interest in this Mother Earth of ours."

In his nice, slick way he was laying it on just a trifle
thick, for over the years there had been many, as he called
them, persons of the arts who had paid attention to the
Earth, and in every case under the very polished and
maternal auspices of Mother Earth itself. Even if one had
not known of the patronage, it could have been suspected.
Most of their work read, looked, or sounded like something
a highly paid press relations outfit would have fabricated to
advertise the Cemetery.

"It is pleasant here," I said, more to be making conversation than for any other reason.

I didn't know that I was asking for it, but I was. He settled down comfortably in his chair, like a brooding hen ruffling out her feathers over a clutch of eggs.

"You heard the pines, of course," he said. "There's a song to them. Even from up here, when a window happens to be open, you can hear them singing. Even after thirty years of hearing them, I listen by the hour. It is the song of an eternal peace that can be achieved in its totality nowhere else but Earth. At times it seems to me that it is not the song of pines and wind alone, nor yet alone the sound of Earth. Rather, it is the song of scattered Man gathered home at last."

"I hadn't heard all that," I said. "Perhaps in time I may. After I have listened a little longer. That is what I'm here for."

I might just as well have kept quiet. He wasn't even listening. He didn't want to listen. He had his piece to speak, his snow-job to be done, and he was intent on that and nothing else.

"For more than thirty years," he said, "I have bent every thinking moment to the great ideals of the Last Homecoming. It is not a job that can be accepted lightly. There have been many men before me, many other managers sitting in this chair, very many of them, and every one of them a man of honor and of sensitivity. It has been my job to carry on their work, but not their work alone. I must, as well, uphold the great traditions that have been fostered through the entire history of this Mother Earth."

He slumped back in his chair and his brown eyes became softer, if possible, and slightly watery.

"At times," he told me, "it is no easy matter. There are so many circumstances against which a man must need contend. There are the insinuations and the whispered rumors and the charges that are hinted, but never brought out in the open so that one might cope with them. I suppose that you have heard them."

"Some of them," I said.

"And believed them?"

13

"Some of them," I said.

"Let's not beat about the bush," he said a little gruffly. "Leave us lay it out. Let us say immediately that Mother Earth, Incorporated, is a cemetery association and Earth a cemetery. But it is not a money-making fraud nor a pious imposition nor a high-pressure sales promotion scheme to retail at tremendous profit large pieces of worthless real estate. Naturally, we operate along accepted business lines. It is the only way to do. It is the only way we can offer our services to the human galaxy. All this calls for an organization that is vaster than one can easily imagine. Because it is so vast, it is necessarily loose. There is no such thing as maintaining tight control over the entire operation. There always exists the chance that we, here in administration, are unaware of a lot of actions we would not willingly condone.

"We employ a large corps of public relations specialists to promote our enterprise. We necessarily must advertise to the far corners of the areas peopled by humanity. We cheerfully concede that we have sales representatives on all planets occupied by humans. But all of this can be considered as no more than normal business practice. And you must consider this—that in pushing our business so forcefully we are conferring a great benefit upon the human race on at least two levels."

"Two levels," I said, astonished—astonished by the man rather than by his flow of words. "I had thought . . ."

"The personal level," he said. "That was the one you thought of. And it, of course, is the prime consideration. Believe me, there is a world of comfort in knowing that one's loved ones have been committed, once life is done, to the sacred keeping of the soil of Mother Earth. There is a deep satisfaction in knowing that one's self, when the time shall finally come, also will be laid to rest amid the hills of this lovely planet where mankind first arose."

I stirred uneasily in my chair. I was ashamed for him. He made me uncomfortable and I resented him as well. He must, I thought, consider me an utter fool if he thought that

14

this flow of flowery, syrupy words would lay at rest any doubts I might have of Mother Earth, Inc., and convert me to Cemetery.

"Aside from this," he said, "there is a second level, perhaps of even greater service. We in Mother Earth, I earnestly believe, serve as a sort of glue that holds the concept of the race intact. Without the concept of Mother Earth, Man would have become a footless wanderer. He'd have lost his racial roots. There would have been nothing to tie him to this comparatively tiny speck of matter revolving about a very common star. No matter how slim the cord may be, it seems to me essential that there be something to bind Man together, some consideration that gives all men a certain thing in common. To serve in this wise, what could be better than a sense of personal association with the planet of their racial origin."

He hesitated for a moment and sat there staring at me. He may have expected some response after his fluent exposition of such noble thoughts. If so, I disappointed him.

"So Earth is a vast galactic cemetery," he went on after it became apparent I was not going to respond. "One must understand, however, it is something more than a common burial ground. It is, as well, a memorial and a memory and a tie that makes all mankind one, no matter where the individual man may be. Without our work, Earth long ago would have died from the memory of Man. It is not inconceivable that under other circumstances the star where Man arose might have become by now a matter of great academic concern and pointless argument, with expeditions blindly groping for some shadowy evidence that would help pin down that solar system where mankind got its start."

He tipped forward in his chair and put his elbows on his desk.

"I bore you, Mr. Carson?"

"Not at all," I told him. And it was the truth. He was not boring me. He fascinated me. It seemed impossible that he could, in conscience, believe this flowery rubbish.

15

"Mr. Carson," he said. "But the first name? The first name now escapes me."

"Fletcher," I said.

"Oh, yes, Fletcher Carson. And you, of course, have heard the stories. About how we overcharge, how we fool the people and high-pressure them, and how . . ."

"Some of the stories," I admitted, "have come to my attention."

"And you thought they might be true."

"Mr. Bell," I said, "I do not see the point—"

He cut me off. "There have been certain excesses on the part of some of our representatives," he said. "It may be that at times the enthusiasm of our copywriters may have given rise to advertisements that were somewhat more flamboyant than would be dictated by good taste. But by and large we have made an honest effort to maintain an essential dignity in keeping with the responsibility that has been placed upon our shoulders.

"Every Pilgrim who has visited Mother Earth will testify that there is nothing more beautiful than the developed portions of our project. The grounds are landscaped, in the most tasteful manner, with evergreen and yew, the grass is tended with a loving care and the floral beds are the most exquisite . . . but, Mr. Carson, you have seen all this."

"A glimpse of it," I said.

"To illustrate the kind of trouble we must face," he told me in what seemed a sudden rush of confidence, as if somehow I had betrayed some sympathy, "a salesman of ours in a far sector of the galaxy caused to circulate, several years ago, a rumor that Mother Earth was running out of room and would soon be full and that those families who wished to have their dead interred here would be well advised to immediately reserve those few remaining lots that were still available."

"And that, of course," I said, "could not possibly be true. Or could it, Mr. Bell?"

I knew, of course, that it couldn't be. I was just needling him, but he didn't seem to notice.

16

He sighed. "Certainly it isn't true. Even those persons who heard it should have known it wasn't. They should have known it was a most malicious rumor and have shrugged it off. But a lot of them went running to complain about it and there was a most messy investigation of the whole affair, causing us no end of trouble, both mental and financial. The worst part of it is that the rumor still is reverberating throughout the galaxy. Even now, on some planets out there, it still is being whispered. We try to stamp it out. Whenever it comes to our attention we try to deal with it. We've been emphatic in our denials, but it seems to do no good."

"It still may sell plots for you," I pointed out. "If I were you, I would not try too hard to stamp it out."

He puffed out his cheeks. "You do not understand," he said. "Fairness and utmost honesty have always been our guides. And in view of that we do not feel that we should be held to strict accountability for the actions of that one salesperson. Because of the distances involved and the resultant difficulties in communication, our organization table is, of necessity, a rather loose affair."

"Which brings up the question," I said, "of the rest of Earth, the part of it that is not Cemetery. What might it be like? I am very anxious . . ."

He waved a chubby hand, dismissing not the question only, but the rest of Earth.

"There is nothing there," he said. "Just a wilderness. An utter wilderness. All that is significant on the planet is the Cemetery. For all practical purposes, the Earth is Cemetery."

"Nevertheless," I said, "I would like—" But he cut me off again and went on with his lecture on the trials of operating Cemetery.

"There is always," he declared, "the question of our charges, always with the implication that they are excessive. But let us, for a moment, consider the costs that are involved. The mere cost of maintaining an organization such as ours staggers the imagination. Add to this the cost

17

of operating our fleets of funeral ships, which make their constant rounds to the many planets, gathering in the bodies of the late departed and returning them to Earth. Now add to this the cost of our operations here on Mother Earth and you'll arrive at a total which fully justifies our charges.

"Few family members, you must understand, care to experience the inconvenience necessary to accompany their loved ones on the funeral ship. Even if they did, we could not offer many of them such accommodations. You have had some months of it and you know that traveling on a funeral ship is no luxury cruise. The cost of chartered ships runs too high for all but the very wealthy and the arrival of the Pilgrim ships, which are not cheap to travel on, does not, as a rule, coincide with the arrival of the funeral ships. Since the family members most often are not able to attend the service of commitment to the sacred soil, we must take care of all the traditional considerations. It is unthinkable, of course, that one be given to Mother Earth without an appropriate expression of sorrow and of human loss. For that reason we must maintain a large corps of pallbearers and of mourners. There also are the florists and the grave-diggers, the monument makers and the gardeners, not to forget the pastors. The pastors are a case in point. There are, as you must realize, quite a lot of pastors. In the process of spreading to the stars, mankind's religions have splintered again and yet again, until now there are thousands of sects and creeds. But despite this, it is the proud boast of Mother Earth that no body is placed within the grave without the precise officiation of the loved one's exact and peculiar sect. To accomplish this, we must maintain a great number of pastors, each qualified in his particular faith, and there are many cases where some of those affiliated with the more obscure sects are called upon no more than a couple of times a year. Still, so that they may be available when the need arises, we must pay their salaries all the year around.

"It is true, of course, that we could effect certain economies. We could realize a substantial savings if we used mechanical excavators for the digging of the graves. But here we stand foursquare and solid in a great tradition and in consequence our human grave-diggers number in the thousands. There would be a saving, too, if we were content to use metal markers for the graves, but here, too, we subscribe to tradition. Each marker in the entire cemetery is carved by hand from the very rocks of Mother Earth.

"There is yet another thing which many are prone to pass over without understanding. There will come a day—far distant, but it *will* come—when Mother Earth is filled, when every foot of ground has been consecrated with the beloved dead. Then our income will cease, but there will still remain the duty and the cost of perpetual care. So to this end each year we must add to the fund for perpetual care, insuring that at no time, so long as Earth shall stand, will ruin or neglect obliterate the monuments to the everlasting memory which has been established here."

"This is all very well," I told him, "and I am glad you told me. But would you mind, I wonder, saying why you told me?"

"Why," he said in some astonishment that I should ask, "just to clear the air. To set the record straight. So that you might realize the problems that we face."

"And so that I might know your deep sense of duty and your firm devotion."

"Yes, that as well," he said, quite unabashed and without any shame at all. "We want to show you all there is to see. The pleasant little villages where our workers live, the beauty of our many woodland chapels, the workshops where the monuments are carved."

"Mr. Bell," I said, "I am not here to take a guided tour. I am not a Pilgrim."

"But surely you'll accept the small assistances and the little courtesies it would be our pleasure to extend."

I shook my head, I hope not too mulishly. "I must go on my own. It's the only way that it will work. I and Elmer and the Bronco."

19

"You and Elmer and the what?"

"The Bronco."

"The Bronco. I do not understand."

"Mr. Bell," I said, "you'd have to know the history of the Earth, some of its olden legends, to really understand."

"But the Bronco?"

"Bronco is an old Earth term for horse. A special kind of horse."

"This Bronco is a horse?"

"No, it's not," I said.

"Mr. Carson, I am not entirely sure I understand who you are or what you mean to do."

"I'm a compositor operator, Mr. Bell. I intend to make a composition of the planet Earth."

He nodded sagely, all doubt cleared from his mind. "Oh, yes, a composition. I should have known at once. You have the look of a sensitive. And you could have chosen no better subject or no better place. Here on Mother Earth you'll find the inspiration that is nowhere else. There is a certain fleeting quality to this planet that has so far escaped the telling. There is music in the very warp and weave of it . . ."

"Not music," I told him. "Not entirely music."

"You mean a composition isn't music?"

"Not in this sense. A composition is a great deal more than music. It is a total art form. It includes music, but it includes as well the written and the spoken word, sculpture, painting, song."

"You mean you do all this?"

I shook my head. "Actually I do little of it. Bronco is the one that really does it."

He flapped his hands. "I am afraid," he said, "that I have become confused."

"Bronco is a compositor," I told him. "It absorbs the mood, the visual impact, the underlying nuances, the sounds, the shape, the form. It takes all these and turns out a product. Not an entirely finished product, but the tapes and patterns for the product. I work with it; the two of us

20

work together. For a time, I suppose you could say, I become a part of it. It picks up the basic materials and I furnish interpretation, although not all the interpretation. That also is shared between us. It becomes, I fear, a bit difficult to explain."

He shook his head. "I have never heard of anything like this. It is new to me."

"It is a fairly new concept," I told him. "It was developed on the planet Alden only a couple of centuries ago and has been in the process of refinement every since. No two of the instruments ever are alike. There is always something that can be done to make the next one better. It is an open-ended project when you settle down to design a compositor, which is an awkward name for it, but no one has thought of a better one."

"But you call this one Bronco. There must be something in the name . . ."

"It's like this," I said. "The compositor is rather large and heavy. It is a complex mechanism and there are many rather delicate components that require heavy shielding. It is not something that one could drag around; it has to be self-propelling. So while we were about it, we built a saddle on it so a man could ride."

"By we I suppose you mean yourself and Elmer. How does it happen Elmer is not with you now?"

"Elmer," I told him, "is a robot and he is in a crate. He traveled on board the ship as freight."

Bell moved uneasily, protesting. "But, Mr. Carson, you must know. Surely you must know. Robots are not allowed on Mother Earth. I am afraid we must . . ."

"In this case, you have no choice," I said. "You cannot refuse him entry to the planet. He is a native of the Earth and this is something neither you nor I can claim."

"A native! It's impossible. You must be jesting, Mr. Carson."

"Not in the least. He was fabricated here. In the days of the Final War. He helped build the last of the great war ma-

21

chines. Since then he has become a free robot and, according to galactic law, holds all the rights a human has, with a very few exceptions."

Bell shook his head. "I am not sure," he said. "I am not sure at all . . ."

"You need not be sure," I said. "I am. I checked into the law, most thoroughly. Not only is Elmer a native, but in the meaning of the law he is native-born. Not fabricated. Born. Back on Alden there is a very legal document that attests to all of this and I have a copy with me."

He did not ask to see the copy.

"For all intents," I said, "Elmer is a human being."

"But surely the captain would have questioned . . ."

"The captain didn't care," I said. "Not after the bribe I paid him. And in case the law is not enough, I might point out that Elmer is all of eight feet tall and very, very tough. What is more, he is sentient. He wouldn't let me turn him off when I nailed him in the crate. I'd hate to think of what might happen if someone other than myself opened up that crate."

Bell eyed me almost sleepily, but there was a wariness behind the sleepiness. "Why, Mr. Carson," he asked, "do you think so badly of us? We appreciate your coming, your having thought of us. Any aid that Mother Earth can give is yours if you only mention it. If there should be financial problems . . ."

"There are financial problems, certainly. But we seek no aid."

He persisted. "There have been occasions when we extended monetary grants to other persons of the arts. To writers, painters . . ."

"I have tried as plainly as I can," I said, "to indicate that we want no ties to Mother Earth or to the Cemetery. But you deliberately persist in your misunderstanding. Must I put it bluntly?"

"No," he said, "I would think there is no need. You are laboring under a romantic misapprehension there is more to Earth than the Cemetery and I tell you, sir, there is nothing else. Earth is worthless. It was destroyed and abandoned ten thousand years ago and it would have been forgotten long ago if it had not been for us. Will you not reconsider? There would be much mutual benefit to both of us. I am intrigued by this new art form that you have described."

"Look," I said, "you might as well understand this. I don't propose to turn out a Cemetery work. I'm not up for hire as a press agent for Mother Earth. And I owe you nothing. I paid your precious captain five thousand credits to haul us here and . . ."

"Which was less," Bell said angrily, "than you would have paid on a Pilgrim ship. And a Pilgrim ship would not have taken all your freight."

"I thought," I said, "that it was sufficient payment."

I didn't say good-bye. I turned about and left. Walking down the steps of the administration building, I saw a ground car was parked in front of the steps, in the traffic circle. It was the only car in sight. The woman who sat in it was looking straight at me, as if she might have known that I was in the building and had been waiting for me.

The car was a screaming pink and that color, pink, made my thoughts go back to Alden, where it all had started.

3

It had been early evening and I'd been in the garden watching the purple cloud that hung above the pink horizon (for Alden was a pink world), listening to the evensong of the temple birds that had gathered in the little grove of trees at the garden's foot. I was listening with some pleasure, when trampling down the dusty path that led across the pink and sandy plain came this great eight-foot monstrosity, lurching along with his awkward stride like a drunken behemoth. Watching him, I hoped that he would pass by and leave me with the evening and the birds, for I was in no mood for strangers. I was considerably de-pressed and there was nothing I wanted quite so much as to be left alone so I'd have a chance to heal. For this had been the day when I'd finally come face-to-face with hard reality and had known that the dream of Earth was dead unless I could get more money. I knew how little chance I had of getting money. I had scraped up all I could and borrowed all I could and would have stolen if there'd been any chance of stealing. I'd had a hard look at it all and knew I wasn't going to be able to build the kind of compositor I wanted and the sooner I got reconciled to all of this, the better it would be.

I sat in the garden and watched this great monstrosity lurching down the path and I tried to tell myself that he was headed elsewhere and would not stop. But that was purely wishful thinking, for my garden was the only place he could be heading for.

He looked like a worker robot, perhaps a heavy construction robot, although what a heavy construction robot would be doing on a planet such as Alden I could not imagine. Heavy construction is just one of the many things that are not done on Alden.

He came lurching up and stopped beside the gate. "With your permission, sir," he said.

"Welcome to my home," I told him, through my teeth.

He unlatched the gate and came through, stopping to make sure it was latched again before coming on. He came over to me and hunkered down as gently as he could and hissed a little at me as a matter of politeness. Have you ever heard a three-ton robot hiss? I tell you, it's uncanny.

"The birds are doing nicely," said this hunk of metal, squatting there beside me.

"They do very well," I said.

"Allow me," said the robot, "to introduce myself."

"If you would please," I said.

"My name is Elmer," said the robot. "I am a free machine. I was given freedom papers many centuries ago. I have been my own man ever since."

"Well," I said, "congratulations. How are you making out?"

"Very well," said Elmer. "I just sort of wander, going here and there."

I nodded, believing him. You saw them now and then, these free and wandering robots who had gained, technically, the status of a human after many years of servitude.

"I have heard," said Elmer, "that you're going back to Earth."

Not to the Earth, but back to Earth—that was the way of it. After more than ten millennia, one still went back to Earth. As if the human race had left it only yesterday.

"You have been misinformed," I said.

"But you have a compositor . . ."

"A basic instrument," I told him, "that needs a million things to do the kind of job that should be done. It would be pitiful to go to Earth with such a pile of junk."

25

"Too bad," said Elmer. "There is a glorious composition waiting on the Earth. There is only one thing, sir . . ."

He stuttered to a halt, embarrassed for some reason I could not detect. I waited, not wishing to further embarrass him by saying anything.

"What I meant to say, sir—and it may not be in my province to say anything at all—is that you must not allow yourself to be trapped by the Cemetery. The Cemetery is no part of the Earth. It is something that has been grafted on the Earth. Grafted, if I may say so, with a colossal cynicism."

I pricked up my ears at that. Here, I told myself with more surprise than I would admit, was someone who was in agreement with me. I took a closer look at him in the gathering dusk. He wasn't much to look at. His body was old-fashioned, at least by Alden standards, a clumsy thing, all brawn, an unsoftened lusty body, and his head piece was one upon which no effort had been expended to make it sympathetic. But rough and tough as he might seem, his speech was not the kind of language one would expect from a hulking, outdated labor robot.

"I am somewhat surprised," I told him, "and at the same time gratified, to find a robot who has an interest in the arts, especially in an art so complicated."

"I have tried," said Elmer, "to make myself a whole man. Not being a man, I suppose, might explain why I tried so hard. Once I got my freedom papers and was given in the process the status of a human, I felt it incumbent on myself to try to be a human. It's not possible, of course. There is a great deal of machine still left in me . . ."

"But composition work," I said, "and myself—how did you know I was at work on an instrument?"

"I am a mechanic, see," said Elmer. "I've been a mechanic all my life, by nature. I look at a thing and I know instinctively how it works or what is wrong with it. Tell me what kind of machine you want built and the chances are that I can build it for you. And when you come right down to it, a compositor is about as complicated a piece of mechanism as one can happen on and, more than that, it is far from finished yet. It is still in the process of development and there is no end to the ways that one can go. I see you looking at these hands and wondering how I can do the kind of work a compositor requires. The answer is that I have other hands, very special kinds of hands. I screw off my everyday hands and screw on whatever other kind is needed. You have heard of this, of course?"

I nodded. "Yes. And specialized eyes, I suppose you have those as well."

"Oh, yes, indeed," said Elmer.

"You find a compositor a challenge to your mechanical ability?"

"Not a challenge," said Elmer. "That's a foolish word to use. I find satisfaction in working with complicated mechanisms. It makes me more alive. It makes me feel worthwhile. And you asked how I heard about you. Well, just a passing remark, I guess—that you were building a compositor and planned to go back to Earth. So I inquired around. I found out you had studied at the university, so I went there and talked to people. There was one professor who told me he had great faith in you. He said you had the soul for greatness, he said you had the touch. His name, I think, was Adams."

"Dr. Adams," I said, "is old now and forgetful and a very kindly man."

I chuckled, thinking of it—of this great, bumbling, earnest Elmer clumping across the fairy campus and stumbling down the venerated, almost sacred halls, hunting out professors from their academic lairs to ask them insistent, silly questions about a long-gone student that many of them, no doubt, had trouble in recalling.

"There was yet another professor," said Elmer, "who impressed me greatly and I had a long talk with him. He was not in the arts, but in archaeology. He said he knew you well."

"That would be Thorndyke. He is an old and trusted friend."

"That's the name," said Elmer.

I was a bit amused, but somewhat resentful, too. What business did this blundering robot have to be checking up on me?

"And you are now convinced," I asked, "that I am fully capable of building a compositor?"

"Oh, most assuredly," he said.

"If you have come with the hope of being hired, you have wasted your time," I said. "Not that I don't need the help. Not that I wouldn't like to have you. But I've run out of money."

"It wasn't that entirely, sir. I would, of course, be delighted to work on it with you. But my real reason was I want to go back to Earth. I was born there, you see; I was fabricated there."

"You were what?" I yelled.

"I was forged on Earth," said Elmer. "I'm a native of the Earth. I would like to see the planet once again. And I thought that if you were going . . ."

"Once again," I said, "and slow. Do you really mean that you were forged on Earth? In the olden days?"

"I saw the last of Earth," said Elmer. "I worked on the last of the war machines. I was a project manager."

"But you would have worn out," I said. "You would be worn out by now. A robot can be long-lived, of course, but . . ."

"I was very valuable," Elmer pointed out. "Ship room was found for me when men began going to the stars. I was not just a robot. I was a mechanic, an engineer. Humans needed robots such as I to help establish their new homes far in space. They took good care of me. Worn parts were replaced, I was kept in good repair. And since I gained my freedom I have taken good care of myself. I have never bothered with the external body. I have never changed it. I have kept it free of rust and plated, but that is all. The body does not count, only the internal working parts. Although now it is impossible to get shelf replacements. They are no longer in stock, but must be placed on special order."

What he said had the ring of truth to it. In that long-gone moving day when, in a century or so, men had fled the Earth, a wrecked and ruined planet, because there was nothing left to keep them there, they would have needed robots such as Elmer. But it was not only this. Elmer had the sound of truth in him. This was no tall tale, I am sure, to impress the listener.

And here he sat beside me, after all the years, and if I would only ask him, he could tell me of the Earth. For it all would still be with him—all that he had ever seen or heard or known would be with him still, for robots do not forget as biologic creatures do. The memories of the ancient Earth would be waiting within his memory core, waiting to be tapped, as fresh as if they had been implanted only yesterday.

I found that I was shaking—not shaking outwardly, physically, but within myself. I had tried to study Earth for years and there was so little left to study. The records and the writings had been lost and scattered, and in those cases where they still existed it was often in only fragmentary form. In that ancient day when men had left the Earth, fleeing for the stars, they had gone out too fast to give much thought to the preservation of the heritage of the planet. On thousands of different planets some of that heritage might still remain, preserved because it had been forgotten, hidden in old trunks or packing boxes tucked beneath the eaves. But it would take many lifetimes for one to hunt it out and even could one find it, more than likely a good part of it would be disappointing—mere trivia that would have no actual bearing on the questions that bobbled in one's mind.

But here sat a robot that had known the Earth and could tell of Earth—although perhaps not as much as one might hope, for those must have been desperate, busy days for him and with much of Earth already gone.

I tried to frame a question and there was nothing I could think of that it seemed that he could answer. One after another the questions came to mind and each one was rejected because it did not fit into the frame of reference of a robot engaged in building war machines.

And while I tried to form a proper question he said something that knocked the questions completely from my mind.

"For years," he said, "I have been wandering around from one job to another and the pay was always good. There's nothing, you understand, that a robot really needs, that he'd feel called to spend his money on. So it has just piled up. And here finally is something I'd like to spend it on. If you would not be offended, sir . . ."

"Offended about what?" I asked, not entirely catching the drift of all his talk.

"Why," he said, "I'd like to put my money into your compositor. I think I might have enough that we could finish it."

I suppose I should have got all happy, I should have leaped to my feet and shouted out my joy. I just sat cold and stiff, afraid to move, afraid that if I moved I might scare it all away.

I said, still stiff and cold, "It's not a good investment. I would not recommend it."

He almost pleaded with me. "Look, it is not just the money. I can offer more than that. I'm a good mechanic. Together, the two of us could put together an instrument that would be the best one ever made."

4

As I came down the steps, the woman sitting at the wheel of the pink car spoke to me.

"You are Fletcher Carson, are you not?"

"Yes," I said, completely puzzled, "but how did you know that I was here? There is no way you could have known."

"I've been waiting for you," she said. "I knew you'd be on the funeral ship, but it took so long to get here. My name is Cynthia Lansing and I must talk with you."

"I haven't too much time," I said. "Perhaps a little later."

She was not exactly beautiful, but there was, even at first sight, something engaging and extremely likable about her. She had a face that fell just short of being heart-shaped, her eyes were quiet and calm, her black hair fell down to her shoulders; she wasn't smiling with the lips, but her entire face was ready to break into a smile.

"You're going out to the shed," she said, "to uncrate Elmer and Bronco. I could drive you out there."

"Is there anything," I asked, "that you don't know about me?"

She did smile then. "I knew that as soon as you got in you'd have to pay a courtesy call on Maxwell Peter Bell. How did you make out?"

"In Maxwell Peter's book I achieved the rating of a heel."

"Then he didn't take you over?"

I shook my head. I didn't quite trust myself to speak.

31

How the hell, I wondered, could she know all she seemed to know? There was only one place she could have learned any of it at all—on Alden at the university. Those old friends of mine, I told myself, might have hearts of gold, but they were blabbermouths.

"Come on, get in," she said. "We can talk on the way out to the shed. And I want to see this wondrous robot, Elmer."

I got into the car. There was an envelope lying in her lap and she handed it to me.

"For you," she said.

It had my name scrawled across the face of it and there was no mistaking that misshapen scrawl. Thorney, I told myself. What the hell did Thorney have to do with Cynthia Lansing ambushing me as soon as I got to Earth?

She started up the car and headed down the driveway. I ripped the letter open. It was a sheet of official University of Alden stationery and in the upper left-hand corner was neatly printed: William J. Thorndyke, Ph.D., Department of Archaeology.

The letter itself was in the same scrawl as the name upon the envelope. It read:

Dear Fletch:

The bearer of this letter is Miss Cynthia Lansing and I would impress upon you that whatever she may tell you is the truth. I have examined the evidence and I would pledge my reputation that it is authentic. She will be wanting to accompany you on your trip and I would take it as the greatest favor you could do me if you should bear with her and supply her with all cooperation and assistance that is possible. She will be taking a Pilgrim ship to Earth and should be there and waiting for you when you arrive. I have placed some departmental funds at her disposal and you are to make use of them if there is any need. All that I need tell you is that her presence on the Earth has to do with what we talked about that last time, when you came to see me just before you left.

I sat with the letter in my hand and I could see him as he had been on that last time I had seen him, in the fire-lit littered room that he called his study, with books shelved to the ceiling, with the shabby furniture, the dog curled upon the hearth rug, the cat upon its cushion. He had sat on a hassock and rolled the brandy glass between his palms, and he had said, "Fletch, I am certain I am right, that my theory's right. The Anachronians were not galactic traders, as so many of my colleagues think. They were observers; they were cultural spies. It makes a deal of sense when you look at it. Let us say that a great civilization had the capacity to roam among the stars. Let us say that in some manner they could spot a planet where an intellectual culture was rising or about to rise. So they plant an observer on that planet and keep him there, alert to developments that might be of value. As we know, cultures vary greatly. This can be observed even among the human colonies that were planted from the Earth. Even a few centuries are enough to provide some variations. The variations are much greater, of course, among those planets that still have or at one time had alien cultures—alien as opposed to human. No two groups of intelligences ever go at anything in parallel manner. They may arrive, eventually, at the same result, or at an approximation of the same result, but they go about it differently, and in the process each develops some capability or some concept which the other does not have. Even a great galactic culture would have developed in this fashion, and because it did develop in this fashion there would be many approaches, many concepts, many abilities which it bypassed or missed along the way. It would seem, this being true, that it would have been worth the while of even our great galactic culture to learn about and have at hand for study those cultural developments it had missed, perhaps had never even thought of. Probably not more than one in ten of these missed developments would be applicable to their culture, but that one in ten might be most important. It might give a new dimension, might make them a more well-rounded and more solid culture. Let us say, which is not true, of course, that Earth had been the only culture that dreamed up the wheel. Even the great galactic culture had missed the wheel, had gone on to its greatness on some other principle that left the lack of the wheel unnoticed. Still, would it not seem likely that knowledge of the wheel, even at a much later date, might be of value? The wheel is such a handy thing to have."

I came back to the present. I still clutched the letter in my hand. The car was nearing the shed. The funeral ship stood on its pad, but there was no sign of the vehicles that had been unloading the cargo. The work must all be done.

"Thorney says that you are expecting to go with us," I said to Cynthia Lansing. "I don't know if that'll be possible. We'll be roughing it. Camping out in all kinds of weather."

"I can rough it. I can camp."

I shook my head.

"Look," she protested, "I gambled everything I had on this, to be here when you landed. I scratched up every credit that I had to pay the outrageous fare on a Pilgrim ship . . ."

"Thorney said something about some funds. A grant."

"I didn't have quite enough for the fare," she said. "I used part of it for that. And I've been waiting for you to arrive, staying at the Pilgrim Inn, which isn't cheap. There is very little left. Really, nothing left . . ."

"That's too bad," I said. "But you knew it was a gamble. You had no reason to believe . . ."

"But I did," she said. "You are as broke as I am."

"Meaning what?"

"Meaning you haven't got the money to get back to Alden once you have your composition."

"I know that," I said, "but if I have the composition . . ."

"No money," she said, "and Mother Earth not about to make it easy for you."

"There is that," I said, "but I can't see how taking you along . . ."

"That is what I have been trying to tell you. This may sound silly to you . . ."

Her words ran out and she sat there looking at me. Her face no longer looked as if it were about to smile.

"Damn you," she said, "why don't you say something? Why don't you help me just a little? Why don't you ask me what I have?"

"All right. What is it that you have?"

"I know where the treasure is."

"For the love of Christ, what treasure?"

"The Anachron treasure."

"Thorney is convinced," I told her, "that the Anachronians had been on Earth. He wanted me to watch for any possible clues to their being here. It was a fool's errand, of course, as he spelled it out to me. The archaeologists aren't even sure there was such a race. Their planet never has been found. All that had been found are fragments of inscriptions on half a dozen planets, fragmentary inscriptions found among the inscriptions and the sherds of the native culture. Some evidence, although it seems to me shaky evidence, that at one time members of this supposedly mysterious race lived on other planets—perhaps as traders, which is what most archaeologists believe, or as observers, which is what Thorney believes, or for some other reason, neither as traders or observers. He told me all of this, but he never mentioned treasure."

"But there was a treasure," she said. "It was brought from olden Greece to olden America in the Final War. I found an account of it and Professor Thorndyke . . ."

"Start making some sort of sense," I said. "If Thorney is right, they weren't here for treasure. They were here for data, to observe . . ."

"For data, sure," she said, "but what about the observer? He would have been a professional, wouldn't he? A historian, perhaps far more than a historian. He would have recognized the cultural value of certain artifacts—the

35

ceremonial hand axe of a prehistoric tribe, a Grecian urn, Egyptian jewelry . . ."

I crammed the letter into my jacket pocket, jumped out of the car. "We can talk about this later," I said. "Right now I have to turn Elmer loose so we can start setting up the Bronco."

"Am I going with you?"

"We'll see," I said.

How the hell, I wondered, could I keep her from going? She had Thorney's blessing; she maybe did have something about the Anachronians, perhaps even about a treasure. And I couldn't leave her here, flat broke—for if she wasn't quite broke yet, she would be if she stayed on at the inn and there was no place else for her to stay. God knows, I didn't want her. She would be a nuisance. I was not on a treasure hunt. I had come to Earth to put together a composition. I hoped to capture some of the feel of Earth—Earth minus Cemetery. I couldn't go off chasing treasure or Anachronians. All that I'd ever told Thorney was that I'd keep my eyes open for clues and that didn't mean going out to hunt for them.

I headed for the open door of the shed, with Cynthia trailing at my heels. Inside the shed was dark and I paused for a moment to let my eyes become accustomed to the darkness. Something moved and I made out three men—three workmen from the looks of them.

"I have some boxes here," I said. There were a lot of boxes, the piled cargo off the funeral ship.

"Right over there, Mr. Carson," said one of them. He gestured to one side and I saw them—the big crate enclosing Elmer and the four crates in which we had boxed the Bronco.

"Thanks," I said. "I appreciate your keeping them separate from the rest. I'd asked the captain, but . . ."

"There's just one little matter," said the man. "Handling and storage."

"I don't get it. Handling and storage?"

"Sure, the charges. My men don't work for free."

"You're the foreman here?"

"Yeah. Reilly is the name."

"How much is this storage?"

Reilly reached into his back pocket and hauled forth a paper. He studied it fixedly, as if making sure he had the figures right.

"Well," he said, "it runs to four hundred and twenty-seven credits, but let us say four hundred."

"You must be wrong," I told him, trying to keep my temper. "All you did was unship the crates and haul them in here and, as for storage, they've been here only an hour or so."

Reilly shook his head, sadly. "I can't help that. Them's the charges. You either pay them or we hold the cargo. Them's the rules."

The other two men had moved up silently, one to either side of him.

"It's all ridiculous," I protested. "This must be a joke."

"Mister," said the foreman, "it isn't any joke."

I didn't have four hundred credits and I wouldn't have paid it if I had, but neither was I going to tackle the foreman and the husky stevedores standing with him.

"I'll look into this," I said, trying to save face, having no idea what I could do next. They had me cold, I knew. Although it wasn't them; it was Maxwell Peter Bell. He was the one who had me cold.

"You do that, mister," said Reilly. "You just go ahead and do it."

I could go storming back to Bell and that was exactly what he wanted. He expected that I would and it would be all right, of course, and all would be forgiven, if I accepted a Cemetery grant and did Cemetery work. But I wasn't going to do that, either.

Cynthia said, behind me, "Fletcher, they're ganging up on us."

I turned my head and there were more men, coming in the door.

"Not ganging up on you," said Reilly. "Just making sure

that you understand. There can't be no outlander come in here and tell us what to do."

From behind Reilly came a faint, thin, screeching sound and the instant that I heard it, I pegged it for what it was, a nail being forced out of the wood that held it.

Reilly and his henchmen swung around and I let out a yell. "All right, Elmer! Out and at them!"

At my yell the big crate seemed to explode, the planks nailed across its top wrenched and torn away, and out of the crate rose Elmer, all eight feet of him.

He stepped out of the crate, almost fastidiously.

"What's the matter, Fletch?"

"Go easy on them, Elmer," I said. "Don't kill them. Just cripple them a little."

He took a step forward and Reilly and the two men backed away.

"I won't hurt them none," said Elmer. "I'll just brush them off. Who's that you got there with you, Fletch?"

"This is Cynthia," I said. "She'll be going with us."

"Will I?" Cynthia asked.

"Look here, Carson," Reilly roared, "don't you try no rough stuff . . ."

"Get going," Elmer said. He took a rapid step toward them and swung his arm. They broke and ran, piling out the door.

"No, you don't!" yelled Elmer. He went past us rapidly. They were closing the door and just before it closed, he thrust a hand into the crack, clutched the door, and wrenched it open, then butted it with his shoulder. It crumpled and hung.

"That will hold them," Elmer said. "Now the door won't close. They were about to lock us in, can you imagine that. Now if you'll tell me, Fletch, what is going on."

"Maxwell Peter Bell," I said, "doesn't like us. Let's get going on the Bronco. The quicker we are out of here . . ."

"I have to get the car," said Cynthia. "I've got all the supplies and my clothes in there."

"Supplies?" I asked.

"Sure. Food and the other stuff we'll need. I don't suppose you brought anything along. That's one reason I'm so broke. I spent the last of my money . . ."

"You go and get the car," said Elmer. "I'll keep watch. There won't no one lay a hand on you."

"You thought of everything," I said. "You were pretty sure . . ."

But she was running out the door. There was no sign of Reilly or his men. She got into the car and drove it through the door into the shed.

Elmer went over to the other crates and rapped on the smaller one. "That you, Bronco?" he asked. "You inside of there?"

"It's me," said a muffled voice. "Elmer, is that you? Have we reached the Earth?"

"I didn't know," said Cynthia, "that Bronco was a sentient thing or that he could talk. Professor Thorndyke didn't tell me that."

"He is sentient," said Elmer, "but of low intellect. He is no mental giant."

He said to Bronco, "You come through all right?"

"I am fine," said Bronco.

"We'll have to get a pinch bar to open up those crates," I said.

"There is no need," said Elmer. He balled a fist and smashed it down on one corner of the crate. The wood crumpled and splintered and he reached his fingers into the resultant hole and tore loose a board.

"This is easy," he grunted. "I wasn't sure I could bust out of my crate. There wasn't too much room and little leverage. But when I heard what was going on . . ."

"Is Fletch here?" asked Bronco.

"Fletch takes care of himself real good," said Elmer. "He is here and he's picked up himself a girl."

He went on ripping boards off the crate.

"Let's get to work," he said.

We got to work, the two of us.

Bronco was a complicated thing and not easy to

39

assemble. There were a lot of parts and all of them had to be phased together with little tolerance. But the two of us had worked with Bronco for almost two years and we knew him inside out. At first we'd used a manual, but now there was no need of one. We'd thrown away the manual when it had become so tattered it was of little use, and when Bronco, himself, refined and redesigned and tinkered here and there, had become a contraption that bore but small resemblance to the model of the manual. The two of us, working together, knew every piece by heart. We could have field-stripped Bronco and put him back together in the dark. There was no waste motion and no need of conference or direction. Elmer and I worked together like two machines. Inside of an hour we had Bronco put together.

Assembled, he was a crazy thing to look at. He had eight jointed legs that had an insect look about them. Each of them could be positioned at almost any angle. There were claws he could unsheathe to get a better grip. He could go anywhere, on any kind of ground. He could damn near climb a wall. His barrel-like body, equipped with a saddle, afforded good protection to the delicate instruments that it contained. It carried a series of rings that allowed the strapping of loads upon his back. He had a retractable tail that was made up of a hundred different sensors and his head was crowned with another weird sensor assembly.

"I feel good," he said. "Are we leaving now?"

Cynthia had unloaded the supplies from the car.

"Camping stuff," she said. "Concentrated food, blankets, rain gear, stuff like that. Nothing fancy. I didn't have the money to buy fancy stuff."

Elmer began heaving the boxes and crates on Bronco's back, cinching them in place.

"You think you can ride him?" I asked Cynthia.

"Sure I can. But what about yourself?"

"He's riding me," said Elmer.

"No, I'm not," I said.

"Be sensible," said Elmer. "We may have to run for it to get out of here. They may be laying for us."

Cynthia went to the door and looked out. "There's no one in sight," she said.

"How do we get out of here?" asked Elmer. "The quickest way out of the Cemetery."

"You take the road west," she told him. "Past the administration building. Twenty-five miles or so and the Cemetery ends."

Elmer finished packing the supplies on Bronco. He took a final look around. "I guess that's all," he said. "Now, miss, up on Bronco."

He helped her up. "Hang on tight," he cautioned her. "Bronco's not the smoothest thing to ride on."

"I'll hang on," she said. She looked scared.

"Now you," Elmer said to me. I started to protest, but didn't because I knew it would do no good. And, besides, riding Elmer made a lot of sense. If we should have to run for it, he could go ten times faster than I could. Those long metal legs of his could really eat up ground.

He lifted me and put me on his shoulders, straddle of his neck. "You hang onto my head to balance yourself," he said. "I'll hold onto your legs. I'll see you don't fall off."

I nodded, not too happy. It was damned undignified.

We didn't have to run for it. There was no one around except one plodding figure far to the north walking down an aisle between the stones. There must have been people watching us; I could almost feel their eyes. We must have made a strange sight—Cynthia riding that grasshopper of a Bronco, with bales and boxes tied all over him, and myself up there, jiggling and swaying atop the eight-foot Elmer.

We didn't run or even hurry, but we made good time. Bronco and Elmer were good travelers. Even at their normal walking pace, a man would have had to run to keep up with them.

We went clattering and lurching up the road, past the administration building and out into the main part of the Cemetery. The road was empty and the land was peaceful. Occasionally, far off, I would sight a little village, nestled in a cove—a slender finger of a steeple pointing at the sky

41

and a blur of color that was the rooftops of the houses. I imagined those little villages were the homes of workers employed by the Cemetery.

As I rode along, bouncing and swaying to Elmer's swinging strides, I saw that the Cemetery, for all its vaunted beauty, was in reality a dismal, brooding place. There was a sameness to it and an endless order that was monotonous, and over all of it hung a sense of death and great finality.

I hadn't had time to worry before, but now I began to worry. What worried me the most, strangely enough, was that Cemetery, after a fairly feeble effort, had made no real attempt to stop us. Although, I told myself, if Elmer had not been able to burst out of his crate, Reilly and his men would have stopped me cold. But as it was, it almost seemed that Bell figured he could let us go, knowing that any time he wished he could reach out and grab us. I didn't try to fool myself about Maxwell Peter Bell.

I wondered, too, if any further attempts would be made upon us. Perhaps there didn't have to be; more than likely Bell and Cemetery might be no longer too much concerned with us. We could go wherever we wished and it would make no difference. For no matter where we went or what we did, there was no chance of leaving Earth without Cemetery's help.

I had made a mess of it, I told myself. I had gone in and played smart-aleck to Bell's pompousness and had thrown away any chance I had of any sort of working relationship with Bell or Cemetery. Although, I realized, it might have made no difference no matter what I'd done. I should have realized that on Earth you played along with Cemetery or you did not play at all. The whole damn venture had been doomed from the very start.

It hadn't seemed so long to me, although it may have been quite a while—I had been so sunk in worry I'd lost all track of time—but finally the road climbed up a hill and there came to an end, and the end of the Cemetery as well.

I stared at the valley below us and the hills that climbed in seried ranks above it, sucking in my breath in astonish-

42

ment at the sight of it. It was a strangely wooded land dressed in flaming color that shone like glowing fires in the sun of afternoon.

"Autumn," Elmer said. "I had forgotten that Earth had autumn. Back there you couldn't tell. All the trees were green."

"Autumn?" I asked.

"A season," Elmer told me. "A certain time of year when all the trees are colored. I had forgotten it."

He twisted his head around so he could look up at me. If he could have wept, he would have.

"One forgets so many things," he said.

5

It was a world of beauty, but of lusty, two-fisted, brooding beauty unlike the delicate, almost fragile beauty of my world of Alden. It was solemn and impressive and there was a dash of wonder and a streak of fear intertwined into the structure and the color of it.

I sat on a moss-grown boulder beside a brawling, dark-brown stream that carried on its surface the fairy boats of red and gold and yellow that were the fallen leaves. If one listened sharply he could pick out, at the edge of the throaty gurgle of the dark-brown water, the faint, far-off pattering of other leaves falling to the earth. And for all the color and the beauty, there was an ancient sadness there. I sat and listened to the liquid sliding of the water and the faint patter of the leaves, and looking at the trees, I saw that they were massive growths, exuding a sense of age, and that there was something secure and homelike and comfortable about them. There was color here and mood and sound, quality and structure, and a texture that could be felt with the fingers of the mind.

The sun was setting, throwing a fog-like dusk across the stream and trees, and there was a coolness in the air. It was time, I knew, to be getting back to camp. But I did not want to move. For I had the feeling that this was a place, once seen, that could not be seen again. If I left and then came back it would not be the same; no matter how many times I might return to this particular spot the place and feeling would never be the same, something would be lost or something would be added, and there never would exist

44

again, through all eternity, all the integrated factors that made it what it was in this magic moment.

A stone rattled behind me and I turned to see that it was Elmer, moving through the dusk. I said nothing to him and he did not speak to me, but came and squatted down beside me and there was nothing to be said, nothing that needed to be said. I sat there, remembering all the other times like this—when there had been no need of words between Elmer and myself. We sat as the twilight deepened and from far away came the sound of something hooting and a little later the faint sound of something that was baying. The water went on talking as the darkness deepened.

"I built a fire," said Elmer, finally. "We'll need it for cooking, but even if we had no need of it, I still would have built fire. The Earth calls for a fire. The two of them go together. Man came up from savagery with fire. In all of man's long history he never let the fire go out."

"Is it," I asked, "the way you remember it?"

He shook his head. "Not the way I remember it, but somehow it is the way that I knew it would be. There weren't trees like these, or a stream like this. But you see one tree flaming in the autumn sun and you can imagine what it might be like with a forest of such trees. You see a stream run red and choked with filth and you know how it might be if the land were clean."

The baying sound came again and walked with chilly feet along my spine.

"Dogs," said Elmer, "trailing something. Either dogs or wolves."

"You were here," I said, "in the Final War. It was different then."

"Different," said Elmer. "Most everything was dead or dying. But there were places here and there where the old Earth still remained. Little pockets where the poison and the radiation had not settled in, places that had been struck no more than a glancing blow. Enough to let you know what it had been like at one time. The people were living mostly underground. I worked on the surface, on one of the war machines—perhaps the last such machine that was ever built. Barring the purpose of it, it was a wondrous mechanism and well it might have been, for it was not machine alone. It had the body of a machine, but the brain of it was something else—a melding of machine and man, a robotic brain linked with the brains of men. I don't know who they were. Someone must have known, but I never did. I have often wondered. It was the only way, you see, that a war could still be fought. No human could go to fight that kind of war. So man's servants and companions, the machines, carried on the war. I don't know why they kept on fighting. I have often asked myself. They'd destroyed all there'd ever been to fight for and there was no use of keeping on."

He quit talking and rose to his feet.

"Let's go back," he said. "You must be hungry and so must the young lady. Fletch, I fear I am a bit confused as to why she is along."

"Something about a treasure."

"What kind of treasure?"

"I don't really know. There was no time for her to explain it to me."

From where we stood we could see the flare of the fire and we walked toward it.

Cynthia was on her knees before a bed of coals she had raked off to one side, holding a pot over the coals and stirring with a spoon.

"I hope it's decent," she said. "It's some kind of stew."

"There is no need for you to be doing that," said Elmer, somewhat miffed. "I am, when called upon, a quite efficient cook."

"So am I," said Cynthia.

"Tomorrow," Elmer said, "I'll get some meat for you. I saw a number of squirrels and a rabbit or two."

"We have no hunting equipment," I said. "We brought along no guns."

"We can make a bow," said Cynthia.

46

"No need of guns or bows," said Elmer. "Stones are good enough. I'll pick up some pebbles . . ."

"No one can hunt with pebbles," Cynthia said. "You can't throw straight enough."

"I can," Elmer told her. "I am a machine. I do not rely on muscles or a human eye, which, marvelous as it may be . . ."

"Where's Bronco?" I asked.

Elmer motioned with his thumb. "He's in a trance," he said.

I moved around the fire so I could get a better look at him. What Elmer had said was right. Bronco was standing to one side with all his sensor apparatus out, soaking up the place.

"The best compositor there ever was," said Elmer, proudly. "He took to it like a shot. He's a sensitive."

Cynthia picked up a couple of bowls and dished up the stew. She handed one of them to me.

"Watch out; it's hot," she said.

I sat down beside her and cautiously began to eat. The stew was not too bad, but it was hot. I had to blow upon each spoonful of it to cool it off before I put it in my mouth.

The baying came again, and it was close now, just a hill or two away.

"Those are dogs," said Elmer. "They are chasing something. Maybe there are people here."

"Maybe just a wild pack," I said.

Cynthia shook her head. "No. I asked around a bit when I was staying at the inn. There are people out here in the wilds—or what Cemetery calls the wilds. No one seems to know too much about them, or at least wouldn't talk too much about them. As if they were beneath any human notice. The normal Cemetery-Pilgrim reaction, what you would expect. You got a taste of that reaction, Fletcher, when you went in to see Maxwell Peter Bell. You never told me how it all turned out."

47

"He tried to take me over. I turned him down, not too diplomatically. I know I should have been more polite, but he put my back up."

"It wouldn't have made any difference," she said. "Cemetery is not accustomed to refusal—even to polite refusal."

"Why did you bother with him at all?" asked Elmer.

"It's expected," I said. "The captain briefed me on it. A courtesy call. As if he were a king or prime minister or potentate or something. I couldn't have ducked it very well."

"What I don't understand," Elmer said to Cynthia, "is how you fit into it. Not that you aren't welcome."

Cynthia looked at me. "Didn't Fletcher tell you?"

"He said something about a treasure . . ."

"I suppose," she said, "I'd better tell it all. Because you have a right to know. And I wouldn't want you to think I was a simple adventuress. There is something rather shoddy about an adventuress. Do you want to listen?"

"We might as well," said Elmer.

She was silent for a moment and you could sense her sort of settling down, getting a good grip on herself, as if she faced a difficult task and was determined that she would do it well.

"I am an Alden native," she began. "My ancestors were among the first to settle there. The family history—perhaps a better way to say it is the family legend, for it's not documented—runs back to their first arrival. But you won't find the Lansing name listed among the First Families—the First Families, capitalized. The First Families are those that prospered. My family didn't prosper. Bad management, pure laziness, lack of ambition, hard luck—I don't know what it was, but they stayed poor as church mice. There is a little place, way back in the outland country, that is called Lansing Corners, but that is all there is, that is the only mark my family made on Alden or on Alden history. They were farmers, small tradesmen, laborers; they had no political aspirations; no genius

48

blossomed in them. They were content to do a good day's work and at the end of it to sit on the doorstep of their cottage and drink their beer, chatting with their neighbors, or alone, watching the fabulous Alden sunsets. They were simple people. Some of them, I guess a lot of them, went off-planet with the years, seeking fortunes that I imagine they never found. If they had, the Alden Lansings would have heard of it and the family legends make no mention of it. I imagine those who were left stayed on simply because they hated to leave; there wasn't much there for them, but Alden is a lovely planet."

"It is that," I said. "I came there to attend university. Until now I never quite worked up the nerve to leave."

"Where did you come from, Fletcher?"

"Rattlesnake," I told her. "You have heard of it?"

She shook her head.

"You're lucky, then," I said. "Don't ask. And please go on."

"Myself, I suppose," she said. "A little background on myself. I set out to make something of myself. I would imagine that through the years many of the Lansings did the same, but it came to nothing. As I may come to nothing. It is a little late in the day to do much for the Lansing image. My father died when I was young. He owned a fairly prosperous farm—not an outstanding farm, but one that made a living and a little more. My mother managed it after his death and there was enough to send me to the university. My interest was history. I dreamed that in time I might hold a chair in history and do learned research and write penetrating papers. I did well in my studies. I should have. I spent all my time at them. I missed many of the other things that college life can give you. I recognize that now, but I didn't mind. There was nothing in the world that fascinated me like history. I simply wallowed in it—far places and far people and far times. At night when I was in bed, in the dark, I'd imagine a time machine and travel through far time to those distant places to observe those ancient people. I'd lie there in the dark and imagine that I was

49

lying in my time machine, in those far lands and times and that just beyond the wall of darkened time moved and lived and breathed those people I had come to spy upon and that all about me those great events were happening that form the tide of history. When the time came to specialize, to follow one specific line of study, I found myself drawn irresistibly to the study of the ancient Earth. My adviser warned me against it. He pointed out that the field was narrow and the resource material very limited. I knew that he was right and I tried to reason with myself, but it did no good. I was obsessed with Earth.

"My obsession with the Earth," she said, "I am quite certain, was in part a rapport with the past, a deep concern for the old beginnings. My father's farm was only a few miles from the locality where the first Lansings had settled on Alden, or so the legend ran. Nestled in a little rocky canyon, at a point where it opened on what at one time must have been a wide, rich valley suitable for farming, was an old stone house, or what at one time had been a stone house. Large parts of it had crumbled, the very stones weathering away with time, disturbed by the small shiftings of the ground that would become significant only after many centuries. There were no stories about it. It was not a haunted house. It was too old to be a haunted house. It simply stood there. Time had made it a part of the landscape. It was not noticed. It was too old and self-effacing to attract human notice, although many little wild creatures, I found when I went to visit it, had made it their home. The land on which it stood and the land around it was so poor and worthless that it interfered with nothing, so it had escaped the tearing down and razing that is so common a fate of many ancient things. The area, in fact, is so worn out for any economic use, ruined by centuries of forgotten farming, that it is seldom visited. Legend said—I must admit, a very shaky legend—that it had been, at one time, the residence of a very early Lansing.

"I visited it, I suppose, because of its very oldness. Not because it may have been Lansing, but simply because it was so old—old beyond the memory of man, a structure from the deeper past. I expected nothing from it. The visit, you must understand, was just a holiday, the filling of an empty day. I had known of it, of course, for a long time, and like all the rest, had ignored it. There were many others who knew of its existence and accepted that existence as they would the existence of a tree or boulder. There was nothing to recommend it, nothing at all. Perhaps I would never have thought of it except in passing, or would never have visited it if it had not been for a gradual sharpening of my concern for olden things. Can you understand what I'm saying?"

"I think," I said, "I understand it far better than you may suspect. I recognize the symptoms. I have suffered most acutely from them."

"I went there," she said, "and I ran my hands along the old, roughly hewn stones and I thought of how human hands, long gone in dust, had shaped them and piled them atop another as a refuge against the night and storm, as a home on a newfound planet. Looking through the ancient eyes of the builders, I was able to understand the attraction of the place of building, knowing why they might have chosen this particular place for the building of a house. Protection of the canyon walls from the sweeping winds, the quiet and dramatic beauty of the place, the water from the spring that still ran in a trickle from underneath a hillside rock, the wide and fertile valley (no longer fertile now) spreading just beyond the doorstep. I stood there in their stead and felt as they would have felt. I was, for a moment, them. And it didn't really matter whether they were Lansings or not; they were people, they were the human race.

"I would have been richly repaid for my time in going there if I had walked away right then. The touching of the stone, the evidence of the past would have been quite enough, but I went into the house . . ."

She stopped and waited a moment, as if gathering herself for the telling of the rest of it.

51

"I went into the house," she said, "and it was a foolhardy thing to do, for at any moment a part of it might have come crashing down upon me. Some of the stones were balanced most precariously and the entire thing was unstable. I don't remember that at the time, however, I gave any thought to this. I walked softly, not because of any danger, but because of the sanctity of time that hovered in that space. It was strange, the feeling that I had—or, rather, the conflicting feelings. When I first went into it I felt that I was an invader, an outsider who had no right of being there. I was intruding on old memories, on old lives, on old emotions that should have been left alone in peace, that had been there so long that they had earned the right to be left alone. I went inside, into what had been a rather large room, perhaps what you might call a living room. There was thick dust upon the floor and the dust was marked by the tracks of wild and small things and there was the odor of wild things having lived there through millennia. Insects had spun webs of silk in the corners and some of the older webs were as dusty as the floor. But as I stood there, just inside the doorway, a strange thing happened—a feeling that I had the right to be there, that I belonged there, that I was coming back after a long, long time on a family visit and was a welcome visitor. For blood of my blood had lived there, bone of my bone, and the right of blood and bone is not erased by time. There was a fireplace in one corner. The chimney was gone, fallen long before, but the fireplace remained. I walked over to it and, kneeling down, touched the hearthstone with my fingers, feeling the texture of its surface through the dust. I could see the fireplace's blackened throat, blackened by the old home fires; the soot still there, resisting time and weather, and there was a moment when it seemed I could see the piled logs and the flame. And I said—I don't know if I said it aloud or only in my mind—I said it is all right, I have come back to tell you the Lansings still persist. Never for a moment confused as to whom I might be saying it. I waited for no answer. I did not expect an answer. There was no one there to answer. It was enough that I should say it. It was a debt I owed them."

She looked at me with frightened eyes. "I don't know why I tell all this," she said. "I did not intend to tell it. There is no reason I should tell you; no reason you should hear it. The facts—the facts I could tell in just a few sentences, but it seemed that they must be told in context . . ."

I reached and touched her arm. "There are some facts that can't be stated simply," I told her. "You are doing fine."

"You are certain you don't mind?"

"Not at all," said Elmer, speaking for me. "I am fascinated."

"There's not much more," she said. "There was a doorway, still intact, leading out of the room into the interior of the house and when I went into this room beyond, I saw that it once must have been a kitchen, although only part of it was there. There was a second story to the house, a part of it still standing, although all the roof was gone, having long since caved in on the rest of the structure. But above the kitchen there was no second story. Apparently the eaves of the house had extended over the kitchen and there was a pile of weathered debris lying along what had been the kitchen's outside wall, the debris from the caving eaves. I don't know how I happened to notice it—it was not easily detectable—but extending for a short distance out of one section of the debris was a squareness. It looked wrong; it didn't have the look of debris. It was dust-covered, as was everything in the house. There was no way to know that it was metal. It had no gleam. I guess it must have been the squareness of it. Debris isn't square. So I went over and tugged it out. It was a box, corroded, but still intact—the metal at no point had been broken or worn through. I squatted there on the floor beside it and I tried to reconstruct what had happened to it and it seemed to me that at some time it had been tucked away underneath the eaves, up in the attic, and then somehow was forgotten and

53

that it had fallen when the eaves had fallen, perhaps crashing through the kitchen roof, or perhaps, by that time the kitchen had no roof."

"So that's the story," I said. "A box with a treasure clue . . ."

"I suppose so," she said, "but not quite the way you think. I couldn't get the box open, so I carried it back to my apartment and got some tools and opened it. There wasn't much in it. An old deed to a small parcel of land, a promissory note marked paid, a couple of old envelopes with no letters in them, a canceled check or two, and a document acknowledging the loan of some old family papers to the manuscript department of the university. Not a permanent gift; they were just on loan. The next day I went to Manuscripts and made inquiry. You know how manuscript departments are . . ."

"Indeed I do," I said.

"It took a while, but my status as a graduate student in Earth history and the fact that the papers, after all, were my family's papers finally did the trick. They expected I simply wanted to study them, but by the time they were produced—I think that they had probably been misplaced and may have been difficult to locate—I was so fed up that I filed notice that I was revoking the loan and walked out with them. Which was no way for a devoted history student to behave, of course, but by that time I'd had it. The department threatened me with court action and if they had started action it would have been a lovely mess for someone to untangle, but they never did. Probably they considered the papers worthless, although how they would have known I had no idea. They were a small batch of papers, pretty small potatoes in a place like that. They had been placed in a single envelope and sealed. There was no evidence they had ever been examined; they were all haphazard and mixed up. If they had been examined, they would have been sorted and labeled, but it was fairly evident the original seal never had been broken. The whole bunch of papers had been simply filed away and forgotten."

She stopped talking and looked hard at me. I said nothing. In her own time, she'd get around to it. Maybe she had a reason for telling it like this. Maybe she had to live it all over again, to reexamine it all again, to be certain (once again? How many times again?) that she had not erred in judgment, that what she had done was right. I was not about to hurry her, although, God knows, I was a bit impatient.

"There wasn't much," she said. "A series of letters that shed a little light on the first human colonization of Alden—nothing startling, nothing new, but they gave one the feeling of the times. A small sheaf of rather amateurish poems written by a girl in her teens or early twenties. Invoices from a small business firm that might have been of some slight interest to an economic historian, and a memorandum written in rather ponderous language by an old man setting down a story that he had been told by his grandfather, who had been one of the original settlers from Earth."

"And the memorandum?"

"It told a strange story," she said. "I took it to Professor Thorndyke and told him what I've just told you and asked him to read the memo and after he had read it he sat there for a time, not looking at me or the memo or anything at all and then said a word I'd never heard before—Anachron."

"What is Anachron?" asked Elmer.

"It's a mythical planet," I said, "a sort of never-never land. Something the archaeologists dreamed up, a place they theorize . . ."

"A coined word," said Cynthia. "I didn't ask Dr. Thorndyke, but I suspect it comes from anachronism—something out of place in time, very much out of place. You see, for years the archaeologists have been finding evidence of an unknown race that left their inscriptions on a number of other planets, perhaps on many more other planets than they know, for their fragmentary inscriptions have been found only in association with the native artifacts . . ."

"As if they were visitors," I said, "who had left behind a trinket or two. They could have visited many planets and their trinkets would be found only on a few of them, by sheer chance."

"You said there was a memo?" Elmer asked.

"I have it here," said Cynthia. She reached into the inside pocket of her jacket and brought out a long billfold. From it she took a sheaf of folded paper. "Not the original," she said. "A copy. The original was old and fragile. It would not take much handling."

She handed the papers to Elmer and he unfolded them, took a quick look at them, and handed them to me. "I'll poke up the fire," he said, "so there will be light. You read it aloud so we all can hear it."

The memo was written in a crabbed hand, the hand, most likely, of an old and feeble man. In places the writing was a little blurred, but was fairly legible. There was a number at the top of the first page—2305.

Cynthia was watching me. "The year date," she said. "That is what I took it for and Professor Thorndyke thought the same. It would be about right if the man who wrote it is who I think he was."

Elmer had poked up the fire, pushing the wood and coals together, and the light was good. Elmer said, "All right, Fletch. Why don't you begin?"

So I began:

6

To my grandson, Howard Lansing:

My grandfather, when I was a young man, told me of an event which he experienced when he was a young man of about my age and now that I am as old as he was when he told me of it, or older, I pass it on to you, but because you are still a youngster, I am writing it down so that when you have grown older you may read it and understand it and the implications of it the better.

At the time he related the happening to me he was of sound mind, with no mental and only those physical infirmities which steal upon a man as the years go by. And strange as the tale may be, there is about it, or so it has always seemed to me, a certain logical honesty that marks it as the truth.

My grandfather, as you must realize, was born on Earth and came to our planet of Alden in his middle age. He was born into the early days of the Final War when two great blocs of nations loosed upon the Earth a horror and destruction that can scarcely be imagined. During the days of his youth he took part in this war—as much a part as a man could take, for in truth it was not a war in which men fought one another so much as a war in which machines and instruments fought one another with a mindless fury that was an extension of their makers' fury. In the end

57

with all his family and most of his friends either dead or lost (I don't know which and I'm not sure that he did, either), he finally was among that contingent of human beings, a small fraction of the hordes that once had peopled Earth, that went out in the great starships to people other planets.

But the story he told me had nothing to do with either the war or the going out in space, but with an incident that he did not place at all in time and only approximately in space. I have the impression that it happened when he was still a comparatively young man, although I cannot remember now if he actually told me this or if I have conjectured it from some now forgotten details of the tale itself. I freely admit that there are many parts of it that I have forgotten through the years, although the major facts of it are still sharp within my mind.

Through some circumstance which I have now forgotten (if, in fact, he ever told me), my grandfather found himself in what he called a safe zone, a little area, a pocket of geography in which through some happenstance of location with regard to topography or meteorology, the land was less poisoned, or perhaps not poisoned at all by the agents of the war, and where a man might live in comparative safety without the massive protection that was required in other less fortunate areas. I have said he was not specific as to where this place actually had been, but he did tell me that it was at a point where a small river coming from the north flowed into a larger river, the Ohio.

I gained the impression (although he did not tell me, nor did I question him on the point) that my grandfather at the time was not engaged in any actual task or mission, but that once he found the area, quite by accident, he simply stayed on there, taking advantage of the comparative security that it offered. Which, in view of the situation, would have made uncommonly good sense.

How long he stayed there altogether, I have no idea

nor how long he had been there when the event took place. Nor why, finally, he left. All of which, of course, is extraneous to what actually happened.

But, one day, he told me, he saw the ship arrive. There were, at that time, very few air-traveling ships in existence, most of them having been destroyed, and even if there had been, they would have counted, should they be used as such, as very feeble weapons in the war then being waged. And it was, besides, a ship such as he had never seen before. I remember that he told me the manner in which it differed from ships that he had seen, but the details have grown a little fuzzy in my mind and if I tried to set them down, I know I'd get them wrong.

Being a cautious man, as all men must be in those days, my grandfather hid himself as well as he could manage and kept as close a watch as possible upon what was happening.

The ship had landed on the point of one of the hills that stood above the river and once it had settled five robots came out from it and another person that was not a robot—appearing, indeed, to be a man, but my grandfather, from his hiding place, had the feeling that it was not a man, but something with only the outward appearance of a man. When I asked my grandfather why he might have thought this, he was hard put to put a finger on it. It was not the way he walked nor the way he stood nor, later, the way he talked, but there was a strangeness, perhaps a psychic scent, a subconscious triggering of the brain, that told him that this creature that was not a robot was not yet a man.

Two of the robots walked a short distance from the ship and seemed to stand as sentinels, not facing in the same direction all the time, but turning occasionally as if they were studying or sensing the terrain on every side. The rest of them began unloading a large pile of boxes and what appeared to be equipment.

59

My grandfather thought that he was well hidden. He was crouching in a thicket close beside the stream and was hunkered low against the ground so that his silhouette would have been broken by the branches of the thicket and, besides, it was summertime and the shrubs had leaves.

But in a very short time, even before the ship had been completely unloaded, one of the robots working at the unloading left the hilltop and came down the hillside, walking straight toward where my grandfather was hiding in the thicket. He thought at first that it was only a coincidence that the robot should be walking toward him and he stayed very still, even breathing as shallowly as he could.

It was not coincidence, however. The robot must have known exactly where he was. My grandfather always thought that one of the sentinels had somehow spotted him, perhaps by a thermal reading, and, staying on post itself, had passed the information that there was a watcher.

Arriving at the thicket, the robot reached down, grabbed my grandfather by the arm and jerked him out of there, then marched him up the hill.

My grandfather admitted to me that from this point onward his memory was not consecutive. While the time element of what he did remember seemed to be consecutive, not jumbled chronologically, there were gaps for which he could not account. He was convinced that before he was let go or managed to escape (although both of these, too, are conjectured, for at no time, so far as he could recall, did he have the feeling that he was being held captive) an attempt was made to erase the memories of what had happened from his mind. He believed that for a time the memory erasure was effective; it was only after he arrived on Alden that he began, in bits and pieces, to remember what had happened—as if the events had been submerged, pushed deep into his brain, and

60

came pushing back again only after a number of years.

He did remember talking with the man that seemed to him not to be entirely a man, and the impression that he carried with him was that this creature was soft-voiced and not at all unkind, although he could not remember a single thing that was said between them, with one exception. The man (if it were a man) told him, he recalled, that he had come from Greece (there was at that time no country that was known as Greece, but at one time there had been) where he had lived for long—my grandfather remembered clearly that phrase, "for long," and thought it rather strange that it should be expressed that way. The man also told my grandfather that he had sought out a place where life would not be threatened and thought, from certain measurements or from certain other facts my grandfather did not comprehend, that he had found it there in that place he had landed.

My grandfather also recalled that some of the equipment that had been taken from the ship was employed by the robots to drive a deep shaft into the solid rock which lay beneath the hill and, once the shaft was driven, to hollow out great chambers underground. And once this had been done a small hut, rude on the outside, constructed of timbers and made to look as if it were old and about to tumble down, but its interior well finished to make for comfortable living, was built above the tunnel, which had steps going down to the rock-hewn chambers and a clever trapdoor fixed at the mouth of the tunnel so that, once closed, no one would suspect that it was there.

The boxes which had been unloaded from the ship were carried down into the chambers, except for a few that held furniture and furnishings for the hut atop the tunnel.

When one of the boxes was being carried down the steps into the chambers it slipped out of a robot's grasp and my grandfather, who, for some reason he does not recall, was in the chamber below, saw it come tumbling down the stairs and hurriedly got out of its way. It was a heavy box, but even so, as it tumbled down the stairs, it began to come apart, to be battered apart by striking on the stones, and by the time it reached the bottom of the steps it had come apart entirely so that all that it contained was either scattered on the steps or spilled out on the chamber's floor.

There was a great treasure in that box, my grandfather told me—jewel-encrusted pendants and bracelets and rings, all set with shining stones; small wheels of gold with strange markings on them (my grandfather insisted they were gold, although how he could tell a thing was gold by simply looking at it, I do not understand); figurines of animals and birds made of precious metals and set with precious stones; a half a dozen crowns (the kind kings or queens would wear); bags that split open to loose a flood of coins, and many other things, including some vases, all of which were smashed.

The robots came rushing down the stairs to pick up all the treasure that was scattered and behind them came their master and when he reached the bottom of the stairs he paid no attention to all the other things, but stooped and picked up some of the pieces of a shattered vase and tried to fit them back together, but he could not fit them back together, for they had been broken into too many pieces. But from the few pieces that he did fit together, trying to hold all those broken pieces in their proper places, my grandfather saw that the vase had had painted pictures on it, fired into the glaze—pictures of strange men hunting even stranger beasts, or maybe they only seemed stranger because they were so badly done, with no thought of perspective and without the anatomical knowledge that is basic with an artist.

62

The man (if it were a man) stood there with the broken pieces in his hands and his head was bent above them and his face was sad and a tear rolled down his cheek. My grandfather thought it strange that a man should weep at the sight of a broken vase.

All this time the robots were picking up the stuff and putting it in a pile and one of them went and got a basket and put it all into the basket and carried it off to be stored with all the other boxes in one of the rock-hewn chambers.

But they didn't get it all, for my grandfather, with no one seeing him, picked up a coin and secreted it about his person and I now will wrap this coin, which he passed on to me, and put it in this envelope . . .

7

I stopped reading and looked across the fire at Cynthia Lansing.

"The coin?" I asked.

She nodded. "It was in the envelope, wrapped in a piece of foil, a kind of foil that has not been used for centuries. I gave it to Professor Thorndyke and asked him if he'd keep it . . ."

"But did he know what it was?"

"He wasn't sure. He took it to another man. An expert on old Earth coins and such. It was an uncirculated Athenian owl, probably minted a few years after a battle fought at a place called Marathon."

"Uncirculated?" Elmer asked.

"It had not been used. There was no wear on it. When a coin is circulated it becomes smooth and dull from much handling. But aside from some deterioration due to time, this one was exactly as it had been the day that it was struck."

"And there can't be any doubt?" I asked.

"Professor Thorndyke said there could be none at all."

The baying of the dogs still could be heard beyond the ridge that rose above our camp. It was a lonely and a savage sound and I shivered as I listened to it and moved closer to the fire.

"They are after something," Elmer said. "Maybe coon or possum. The hunters are back there somewhere, listening to the dogs."

"But what are they hunting for?" asked Cynthia. "The men, I mean, the men who sent out the dogs."

"For sport and meat," said Elmer.

I saw her wince.

"This is no Alden planet," Elmer told her. "No planet soft and full of pinkness. The people who live back here in the woods are probably one-half savage."

We sat listening and the baying of the dogs seemed to move away.

"On this treasure business," Elmer said, "leave us try to figure out what we have. Somewhere in this country to the west of us someone came fleeing out of Greece and hid out a bunch of boxes, some of which probably contained treasure. We know one of them did and some of the others may have. But the location might be a little hard to come by. It's indefinite. A river flowing from the north into the old Ohio. There might be quite a lot of streams coming from the north . . ."

"There was a hut," said Cynthia.

"That was ten thousand years ago. The hut must be long gone. We'd be looking for a hole, a tunnel, and that might be covered over."

"What I want to know," I said, "is why Thorney should have thought this strange character out of Greece might be Anachronian."

"I asked him that," said Cynthia, "and he said that Greece or somewhere in that area of the planet would most likely be the place an alien observer would have set up his observation post. The first settled communities of the human race were established in what once was known as Turkey. An observer would not have set up a post too close to what he wished to study. He'd want to be in a position to do some observation and then get out of there. Greece would be logical, Professor Thorndyke said. Such an observer would have had some means of rather rapid transportation and the distance between the first settlements and Greece would have been no problem."

"It doesn't sound logical to me," said Elmer, bluntly.

"Why Greece? Why not the Sinai? Or the Caspian? Or a dozen other places?"

"Thorney goes on hunches as much as evidence or logic," I told them. "He has a well-developed hunch sense. He is very often right. If he says Greece I'd go along with him. Although it would seem this hypothetical observer of ours could have moved location time and time again."

"Not if he were picking up loot all the time," said Elmer. "He'd get weighed down with it. It would be quite a job to move. He probably brought along several tons of it when he moved to the Ohio."

"But it wasn't loot," cried Cynthia. "You have to understand that it wasn't loot. Not loot in terms of money, or in terms of whatever value the Anachronians might employ. Whatever he picked up were cultural artifacts."

"Cultural artifacts," said Elmer, "running very heavily to gold and precious stones."

"Let's be fair about it," I said to Elmer. "It might just have happened that the broken box was filled with that kind of stuff. Some of the other boxes might have been filled with arrowheads or spear points, early woven stuffs, mortars and pestles."

"Dr. Thorndyke thought," said Cynthia, "that the boxes my old ancestor saw contained only a small fraction of what the observer had collected. Probably only a few of the more significant items. Back somewhere in Greece, perhaps in other caverns carved into the rock, there may be a hundred times as much as was in the boxes."

"Whatever it may be it spells out treasure," Elmer said. "Artifacts of any sort command a price and I suppose they'd be worth even more if they were artifacts from Earth. But Earth or not, there is a booming trade in them. A lot of wealthy men, and they have to be wealthy to pay the prices asked, have collections of them. But aside from that, I understand it's chic to have an artifact or two on the mantelpiece or in a display cabinet."

I nodded, remembering Thorney, pacing up and down the room, striking his clenched fist into an open palm and fulminating. "It's getting so," he'd yell, "that an honest ar-chaeologist hasn't got a chance. Do you know how many looted sites we've found in the last hundred years or so—dug up and looted before we ever got to them? The various archaeological societies and some of the govern-ments have made investigations and there is no evidence of who is doing it or where the artifacts are taken to be hidden out. We've found no trace of them or whoever might be responsible. They are looted and warehoused somewhere and then they trickle back into collectors' hands. It's big business and it must be organized. We've pushed for laws to forbid private ownership of any artifact, but we get nowhere. There are too many men in government, too many men who have special interests, who are themselves collectors. And undoubtedly there are funds available, from someone, to fight such legislation. We are simply get-ting nowhere. And because of this vandalism we are losing the only chance we have to gain an understanding of the development of galactic cultures."

The baying of the dogs had changed to excited yapping.

"Treed," said Elmer. "Whatever they were running has taken to a tree."

I reached out to the little pile of wood Elmer had brought in, laid new sticks on the fire, used another to push the spreading coals together. Little tongues of blue-tipped flame ran up from the coals to lick against the new wood. Dry bark ignited and threw out sparks. The fresh fuel caught and the fire leaped into new life.

"A fire is a pleasant thing," said Cynthia.

"Could it be," asked Elmer, "that even such as I should be warmed by such a feeble flame? I swear that I feel warm-er sitting here beside it."

"Could be," I said. "You've had a lot of time to grow in-to a man."

"I am a man," said Elmer. "Legally, that is. And if legally, why not otherwise?"

"How is Bronco getting on?" I asked. "He should be here with us."

"He is sitting out there soaking it all up," said Elmer. "He is weaving a woodland fantasy out of the dark shapes of the trees, the sound of nighttime wind in leaves, the chuckle of the water, the glitter of the stars, and three black shapes huddled at a campfire. A campfire canvas, a nocturne, a poem, perhaps a delicate piece of sculpture—he's putting it all together."

"He works all the time, poor thing," said Cynthia.

"It is not work for him," said Elmer. "It is his very life. Bronco is an artist."

Somewhere off in the dark something made a flat cracking sound, and an instant later it was followed by another. The dogs, which had fallen silent, resumed excited barking.

"The hunter shot whatever it was that the dogs had treed," said Elmer.

After he had spoken, no one said a word. We sat there imagining—or at least I was imagining—that scene off there in the darkened woods, with the dogs jumping about the tree, excited, the leveled gun and the burst of muzzle flame, the dark shape falling from the tree to be worried by the dogs.

And as I sat there listening and imagining, there was another sound, faint, far off—a rustling and a crackling. A breath of breeze came down the hollow and swept the sound away, but when the breeze died down, the sound was there again, louder now and more insistent.

Elmer had leaped to his feet. The flicker of the fire sent ghostly metallic highlights chasing up and down his body.

"What is it?" Cynthia asked and Elmer did not answer. The sound was closer now. Whatever it might be, it was heading toward us and was coming fast.

"Bronco!" Elmer called. "Over here, quick. By the fire with us."

Bronco came spidering rapidly.

"Miss Cynthia," Elmer said, "get up."

"Get up?"

"Get up on Bronco and hang on tight. If he has to run, stay low so a tree branch won't knock you off."

68

"What is going on?" asked Bronco. "What is all the racket?"

"I don't know," said Elmer.

"The hell you don't," I said, but he didn't hear me; if he did, he didn't answer.

The noise was much closer now. It was no kind of noise I had ever heard before. It sounded as if something was tearing the very woods apart. There were popping sounds and the shriek of tortured wood. The ground seemed to be vibrating as if something very heavy was striking it repeated hammer blows.

I looked around. Cynthia was up on Bronco and Bronco was dancing away from the fire out into the dark, not running yet, but staying limber and ready to run at a second's notice.

The noise was almost upon us, shrieking and deafening and the very ground was howling. I leaped to one side and crouched to run and would have run, I suppose, except I did not know where to run, and in that instant I saw the great bulk of whatever it was up on the ridge above us, a huge dark mass that blotted out the stars. The trees were shaking wildly and crashing down to earth, overridden and smashed by the black mass that charged along the ridgetop, almost brushing the camp, and then going away, missing us, with the noise rapidly receding down the hollow. On the ridge above, the smashed-down trees still were groaning softly as they settled into rest.

I stood and listened as the noise moved away from us and in a little time it was entirely gone, but I still stood where I was, half-hypnotized by what had happened, not knowing what had happened, wondering what had happened. Elmer, I saw, was standing, as hypnotized as I.

I sat down limply by the fire, and Elmer turned around and walked back to the fire. Cynthia slid off Bronco.

"Elmer," I said.

He shook his massive head. "It can't be," he mumbled, talking to himself rather than to me. "It would not still be there. It could not have lasted . . ."

"A war machine?" I asked.

He lifted his head and stared across the fire at me. "It's crazy, Fletch," he said.

I picked up wood and fed the fire. I put on a lot of wood. I felt an urgent need of fire. The flames crawled up the wood, catching fast.

Cynthia came over to the fire and sat down beside me.

"The war machines," said Elmer, still speaking to himself, "were built to fight. Against men, against cities, against enemy war machines. They'd fight to the very death, until the last effective ounce of energy was gone. They were not meant to last. They were not fashioned to survive. They knew that and we who built them knew it. Their only mission was destruction. We fashioned them for death, we sent them out to death . . ."

A voice speaking from the past of ten thousand years before, speaking of the old ethics and ambitions, of ancient blood striving, of primordial hate.

"The ones who were in them had no wish to live. They were already dead. They had a right to die and they postponed their dying . . ."

"Elmer, please," said Cynthia. "The ones who were in them? Who was in them? I had never heard that anyone went in them. They had no crews. They were . . ."

"Miss," said Elmer, "they were not all machine. Or at least ours were not all machine. There was a robot brain, but human brains as well. More than one human brain in the one I worked on. I never knew how many. Nor who they were, although we knew they were the still competent brains of competent men, perhaps the most competent of military men who were willing to continue living for a little longer to strike one final blow. Robot brain and human brain forming an alliance . . ."

"Unholy alliance," Cynthia said.

Elmer shot a quick glance at her, then looked back at the fire. "I suppose you could say so, miss. You do not understand what happens in a war—a sort of sublime madness, an

70

unholy hatred that is twisted into an unreasoning sense of righteousness . . ."

"Let us quit all this," I said. "It may have been no war machine. It may have been something else entirely."

"What something else?" asked Cynthia.

"It's been ten thousand years," I said.

"I suppose so," Cynthia said. "There could be a lot of other things."

Elmer said nothing. He sat quietly.

Someone shouted on the ridge above us and we all came to our feet. A light was bobbing up there somewhere and we heard the sound of bodies forcing their way through the swath of fallen trees.

Someone shouted again. "Ho, the fire!" he said.

"Ho, yourself," said Elmer.

The light kept on bobbing.

"It's a lantern," Elmer said. "More than likely the men who were out hunting with the dogs."

We continued to watch the lantern. There was no more shouting at us. Finally the lantern ceased its bobbing and moved down the hill toward us.

There were three of them, tall scarecrow men, grinning, their teeth shining in the flicker of our fire, guns across their shoulders, one carrying something on his back. Dogs frisked about them.

They stopped at the edge of the campfire circle, stood in silence for a moment, looking us over, taking us in.

"Who be you?" one of them finally asked.

"Visitors," said Elmer. "Travelers, strangers."

"What be you? You are not human." He made it sound like "hooman."

"I am a robot," Elmer said. "I am a native of this place. I was forged on Earth."

"Big doings," said another one of them. "Night of big doings."

"You know what it was?" asked Elmer.

"The Ravener," said the first who had spoken. "Old

stories told of it. Great-grandpappy, his father told him of it."

"If it pass you by," said the third one, "no need of fearing it. No man sees it twice in one lifetime. It comes again only after many years."

"And you don't know what it is?"

"It's the Ravener," as if that were all the explanation that was needed, as if no one should ask for more.

"We seen your fire," said the first one. "We dropped by to say hello."

"Come on in," said Elmer.

They came on in and squatted by the fire, their gun butts rested on the ground, the barrels propped against their shoulders. The one who had been carrying something on his back threw his burden to the ground in front of him.

"A coon," said Elmer. "You had good hunting."

The dogs came in and flopped down on the ground panting. Their tails beat occasional polite tattoos.

The three sat in a row, grinning up at us. One of them said, "I am Luther and this is Zeke and the fellow at the end is Tom."

"I am pleased to know you all," Elmer said, speaking as politely as he could. "My name is Elmer and the young lady is Cynthia and this gentleman is Fletcher."

They bobbed their heads at us. "And what kind of animal is that you have?" asked Tom.

"His name is Bronco," said Elmer. "He is an instrument."

"I am glad," said Bronco, "to meet up with you."

They stared at him. "You must not mind any of us," said Elmer. "We are all off-worlders."

"Well, heck," said Zeke, "it don't make no difference. We just saw your fire and decided to come in."

Luther reached into his hip pocket and pulled out a bottle. He flourished it in invitation.

Elmer shook his head. "I can't drink," he said.

I stepped over and reached for the bottle. It was time I did my part; up till now Elmer had done all the talking.

"It's right good stuff," said Zeke. "Old Man Timothy, he was the one who made it. Great one with his squeezings."

I pulled the cork and put the bottle to my lips. It damn near strangled me. I kept from coughing. The booze bounced when it hit my stomach. My legs felt rubbery.

They watched me closely, the grins held tightly in.

"It's a man-size drink," I told them. I took another slug and handed back the bottle.

"The lady?" Zeke asked.

"It is not for her," I said.

They passed the bottle among themselves; I squatted down facing them. They passed the bottle back to me. I had another one. My head was getting a little fuzzy from the three quick drinks, but it was, I told myself, for the common good. There had to be one of us who talked their kind of language.

"Another one?" asked Tom.

"Not right away," I said. "Later on, perhaps. I don't want to drink all your likker."

"I got another in reserve," said Luther, patting a pocket.

Zeke pulled a knife from his belt, reached out and pulled the coon toward him.

"Luther," he said, "you get some green saplings for roasting. We got fresh meat and we got some booze and a good hot fire. Let's make a night of it."

I glanced over my shoulder at Cynthia. Her face was pale and drawn, her eyes watching in horror as Zeke's knife slit neatly down the coon's spread-out belly.

"Easy there," I said.

She flashed a sick smile at me.

"Come morning," said Tom, "we'll go home. Easier to get through the down trees when it's light. Big hoedown tomorrow night. Glad to have you with us. I take it you will come."

"Of course we will," said Cynthia.

I glanced toward Bronco. He was standing rigid, with all his sensors out.

8

He had shown me the fields, with the shocked corn and the pumpkins golden in the sun; the garden, with a few of the vegetables still there, but most of them harvested; the hogs brought in from the woods, fat on acorns and penned for butchering; the cattle and the sheep knee-deep in the meadow grass; the smokehouse ready for the hams and the slabs of bacon; the iron house, in which was stored neatly sorted stacks of different kinds of salvaged metals; the hen house, the tool house, the smithy, and the barns, and now we sat, the two of us, perched on the top rail of a weathered fence.

"How long," I asked him, "have you been here—not you, of course, but the people in this hollow?"

He turned his wrinkled old patriarch face toward me, the mild blue eyes, the beard like so much white silk hanging on his chest. "That's a foolish question to ask of one," he said. "We always have been here. Little clusters of us living all up and down the valley. A few living alone, but not many of them; we mostly live together; a few families that have stuck together farther back than man can remember. Some move away, of course; find a better place, or what they think is a better place. There are not many of us; there never have been many of us. Some women do not bear; many of the youngsters do not live. It is said that there is an ancient sickness in us. I do not know. There are many things said, old tales from the past, but one cannot tell if they are true or not."

He planted his heels more firmly on the second rail,

rested his arms across his knees. His hands were twisted with age. The knuckles stood out like lumps, the fingers stiffly bent. The veins along the backs of his hands stood out in a blue prominence that was startling.

"You get along with the Cemetery people?" I asked.

He considered for a moment before he answered; he was the kind of man, I thought, who always considered well before he answered. "Mostly," he finally said. "Over the years they have crept closer to us, taking over land that, when I was a boy, was wild. Couple of times I've gone and talked to that there fellow . . ." He groped for the name.

"Bell," I said, "Maxwell Peter Bell."

"That's the one," he said. "I go and talk with him, for all the good it does. He is smooth as oil. He smiles, but there is nothing behind the smile. He is sure; he is big and powerful and we are small and weak. You are crowding us again, I tell him, you are moving in on us and there is no need, there is a lot of other land that you can use, a lot of empty land that no one else is using. And he says but you aren't using it and I tell him that we need it, we need it even if we put no plow or hoes to it, we need the land for elbowroom, we've always had a lot of elbowroom, we feel crowded if it isn't there, we feel smothered. And then he says but you have no title to it and I ask him what is a title and he tries to tell me what title is and it all is foolishness. I ask him does he have title to it and he never answers. You come from out there somewhere, mister, maybe you can tell me does he have title to it."

"I doubt it very much," I said.

"We get along all right with them, I guess," he said. "Some of us work for Cemetery every now and then, digging graves, mowing grass, pruning trees and bushes, trimming around the headstones. There's a lot of work to keeping a burying ground looking trim and neat. They use us just now and then, extra hands when the work gets ahead of them. We could work a whole lot more, I guess, if we wanted to, but what's the use of working? We got all we want; there's not much they can offer for our work. Some fancy cloth, at times, but we have all the cloth we need from sheep, enough to cover nakedness, enough to keep us warm. Some fancy likker, but we got all the moonshine that we need and I'm not sure it isn't better than Cemetery likker. Moonshine, if you know your business, has authority and it's got a funny kind of taste a man gets partial to. Pots and pans, of course, but how many pots and pans does a woman need?

"It isn't that we are lazy and no account," he said. "We keep right busy. We farm and fish and hunt. We go out to mine old metal. There are a lot of places, most of them a right long piece from here, where there are mounds that have metal in them. We use it to make our tools and shooting irons. Traders come in from the west or south every now and then to trade their powder and lead for our meal and wool and moonshine—other things, of course, but mostly lead and powder."

He stopped talking and we sat close together, on the top rail, in the mellow sunshine. The trees were flaming bonfires frozen into immobility; the fields were tawny, dotted with cornshocks, spotted by the gold of scattered pumpkins. Down the hill from us, at the smithy, someone was hammering and a curl of smoke trailed up from the forge. Smoke, too, streamed up from the chimneys of the closest houses. A door slammed and I saw Cynthia had come out. She was wearing an apron and carried a pan. She went out into the yard and emptied the contents of the pan into a barrel that was standing there. I waved at her and she waved at me, then went back into the house, the door slamming behind her.

The old man saw me looking at the barrel. "Swill barrel," he said. "We dump potato peelings and sour milk and cabbage leaves into it, all the stuff out of the kitchen we don't need. We feed it to the hogs. Don't tell me you never saw a swill barrel."

"I never knew until right now," I said, "there was such a thing."

"I misbelieve," the old man said, "that I rightly caught

the place you came from and what you might be doing there."

I told him about Alden and tried to explain what our purpose was. I'm not sure he understood.

He waved toward the barnyard where Bronco had been planted a good part of the day. "You mean that there contraption works for you."

"Very hard," I said, "and most intelligently. It is a sensitive. It is soaking in the idea of the barn and haystack, of the pigeons on the roof, the calves running in their pens, the horses standing in the sun. It will give us what we need to make music and . . ."

"Music? You mean like fiddle music?"

"Yes," I said. "It could be fiddle music."

He shook his head, half in confusion, half in disbelief.

"There is one thing I have been wanting to ask you," I said. "About this thing the hunters call the Ravener."

"I don't rightly know," he said, "if I can tell you much of it. It got to be called the Ravener and I've often wondered why that was. It never ravens any that I've heard of. Only danger would be if you were right spang in its path. It doesn't show up often. Mostly far away and no one knowing of it until after it is gone. Last night was the first time it ever came within shouting distance of us. No one I ever heard of ever went to look for it or to track it down. There are some things better left alone."

He hadn't told me all he could, I knew, and I had a hunch that he was not about to, but I tried him, anyhow.

"But there must be stories. Perhaps stories from the olden time. Have you ever heard it might be a war machine?"

He looked at me, startled and afraid. "What machine?" he asked. "What war?"

"You mean that you don't know," I asked, "about the war that destroyed Earth? About how the people went away?"

He didn't answer directly, but from what he said I knew he didn't know—the history of the planet had been lost in the mists of centuries.

77

"There are many stories," he said, "and many of them true and perhaps others of them false. And no man in his right mind will hunt too closely into them. There is the census-taker, the one who counts the ghosts, and I thought that he was only another story until the day I met him. And there's the story of the immortal man and him I've never met, although there are folks who claim they have. There is magic and there is sorcery, but in this place we have neither one of them and we have no wish to. We live a good life and we want it to stay that way and we pay little attention to all the stories that we hear."

"But there must be books," I said.

"Once there might have been," he told me. "I have heard of them, but I've never seen one. I don't know anyone who has. We have none here; I think we never had. Exactly, can you tell me, what are books?"

I tried to tell him and although I am sure he did not entirely understand, he seemed somewhat wonder-struck. And to mask his lack of understanding, he carefully changed the subject.

"Your machine down there," he said, "will be at the hoedown? It will watch and listen?"

"Indeed it will," I said. "It is kind of you to have us."

"There'll be a lot of people, from all up and down the hollow. They'll begin showing up as soon as the sun is set. There'll be music and dancing and big tables will be set with many things to eat. Do you, on your Alden, have gatherings such as this?"

"If not exactly hoedowns," I said, "other events that are very similar."

We went on sitting and I got to thinking that it had been a good day. We had tramped the fields and had husked some ears out of one of the cornshocks so the old man could show me what fine corn they raised; we had leaned our arms on the pigpen fence and watched the grunting porkers, nosing through the rubble on the feeding floor for a morsel they had missed; we had stood around and watched a man work the forge until a plow blade was glowing red, then take it out with tongs and place it on an anvil, with the sparks flying when he hammered it; we had strolled through the coolness of the barn and listened to the pigeons cooing in the loft above; we had talked lazily, as unhurried men will talk, and it had all been very good.

The door of the house opened and a woman stuck her head out. "Henry," she called. "Henry, where are you?"

The old man climbed slowly off the fence. "That is me they want," he grumbled. "No telling what it is. It might be anything. These women get the strangest notions about chores that they want done. You just take it easy while I go see what it is."

I watched him amble down the slope and go into the house. The sun was warm on my back and I knew that I should get down off the fence and move around a bit or find something I could do. I must look silly, I thought, perched upon the fence, and I felt a sense of guilt at not having anything to do nor wanting anything to do. But I felt a strange disinclination to do anything at all. It was the first time in my life I'd not had things piled up and waiting to be done. And I found, with some disgust, that I enjoyed it.

Bronco still was planted in the barnyard, with all his sensors out, and there'd been no sign of Cynthia since she'd gone out to the swill barrel. I wondered where Elmer might be; I'd not seen him all day long. And even as I wondered, I saw him come around the barn. Apparently he saw me almost at once, for he angled up the slope toward me. He came up close before he spoke and he kept his voice low and I sensed that he was troubled.

"I've been out looking at the tracks," he said, "and there is no doubt about it. The thing last night was a war machine. I found some tread marks and there's nothing here that leaves tread marks like that except a war machine. I followed the swath it made and I saw that it turned west. There are a lot of places back in the mountains where a war machine could hide."

"Why would it want to hide?"

79

"I can't imagine," Elmer said. "There is no way of telling how a war machine would think. Human brain and machine brain and they've had ten thousand years to evolve into something else. Fletch, given that much time, what could a brain like that become?"

"Maybe nothing," I said. "Maybe something very strange. If a war machine survived destruction, what would it become? What motive would it have to stay alive? How would it view an environment so different from the one for which it had been made? One strange thing, though. The people here seem to have no fear of it. It's just something they don't understand and the world seems to be filled with things they don't understand."

"They're a strange lot," Elmer said. "I don't like the looks of them. I don't like the feel of any part of it. It strikes me as unlikely those three young coon-hunting bucks would have come strolling in on us last night without some sort of reason. They had to cut across the track made by the war machine to do it."

"Curiosity," I said. "Not much happens here. When something does, like us showing up, they have to find out about it."

"Sure, I know," said Elmer, "but that's not all of it."

"Anything specific?"

"No, nothing like that. Nothing that I can pin down. Just a feeling in the guts. Fletch, let's get out of here."

"I want to stay for the hoedown. So Bronco can get it on the tapes. Soon as it is over, we will leave."

9

The people had started coming, as the old man had said they would, shortly after sunset. They had come alone and in twos and threes and sometimes a dozen of them all together, and now the yard was full of them, crowding around the tables where the food was set. There were others in the house and some men were in the barn passing bottles back and forth.

The tables had been set up late in the afternoon when some of the men had gotten sawhorses out of the lumber shed, setting them up in the yard and putting planks across them. A platform for the musicians had been made in the same manner and now the musicians were seated on it, tuning up their instruments, sawing at their fiddles and plunking their guitars.

The moon hadn't risen yet, but it was lighting the sky in the east and beyond the clearing the trees stood up dark against the lighted sky. Someone kicked a dog and the dog went yelping out into the darkness. A roar of sudden laughter came from a group of men standing to one side of a table, perhaps at the telling of a joke. Someone had started a bonfire and piled a lot of wood on it, and flames, eating up through the wood, were swirling high into the air.

Bronco was standing to one side of the clearing, close to the edge of the forest and the firelight from the bonfire seemed to make him flicker. Elmer was with one of the groups near the table where the food was laid and it seemed that he was engaged in a spirited discussion. I looked for Cynthia, but I didn't see her.

81

I felt a touch upon my arm and when I looked around, the old man, Henry, had come up and was standing by my side. Just then the music struck up and couples began forming for a dance.

"You're standing by yourself," the old man said. The little breeze that was blowing ruffled his whiskers.

"I've just been standing off and looking," I told him. "I've never seen the like before." And, indeed, I never had. There was something wild and primitive and barbaric in the clearing; there was something here that should by now have been bred out of the human race. Here there still existed some of the earthbound mysticism that extended back to the gnawed thigh bone and the axe of flint.

"You will stay with us a while," the old man said. "You know that you'll be welcome. You can stay here with us and carry out the work you plan to do."

I shook my head. "We'll have to think about it. We'll have to make our plans. And thank you very much."

They were dancing now, a set and rather savage dance, but with a certain grace and fluidity, and upon the musicians' platform a man with leathern lungs was calling out a chant.

The old man chuckled. "It is called a square dance. You've never heard of it?"

"I've never heard of it," I said.

"I'm going to dance myself," said the old man, "as soon as I have another drink or two to get lubricated. Come to think of it . . ."

He took a bottle from his pocket and, pulling out the cork, handed it to me. The bottle felt cold to my hands and I put it to my lips and took a slug of it. It was better whiskey than I'd had the night before. It went down smooth and easy and it didn't bounce when it hit the stomach.

I handed the bottle back to him, but he pushed my hand away. "Have another one," he said. "You are way behind."

So I had another one. It lay warm inside of me and I began feeling good.

I handed back the bottle and the old man had a drink. "It's Cemetery whiskey," he said. "It's better than what we can make ourselves. Some of the boys went up to Cemetery this morning and traded for a case."

The first dance had ended and another was getting under way. Cynthia was out with this new set of dancers. She was beautiful with the firelight on her and she danced with a lithesome grace that took me by surprise, although I did not know why I possibly could have thought she would not be graceful.

The moon had risen now and was riding in the sky, and I had never felt so good before.

"Have another one," the old man said, handing me the bottle.

The night was warm, the people warm, the woods were dark, the fire was bright, and Cynthia was out there dancing and I wanted to go out and dance with her.

The set ended and I started to move forward, intending to ask Cynthia if she would dance with me. But before I had gone more than a step or two, Elmer came striding to the space that had been cleared for dancing. He came to the center of it and performed an impromptu jig, and as soon as he did that one of the fiddlers on the platform stood up and began to play, if not a jig, at least a sprightly piece of music and the others all joined in.

Elmer danced. He had always seemed to me a stolid, plodding robot, but now his feet patted rapidly upon the ground and his body swayed. The people formed a ring about him and yelled and hollered at him, clapping their hands in encouragement and appreciation. Bronco moved out from his position at the edge of the woods and ankled toward the circle. Someone, seeing him, cried out and the ring of people parted to let him through. He came into the circle and stood in front of Elmer and began to shuffle and pat the ground with all eight feet.

The musicians were playing wildly now and increased the tempo of the music, and in the circle Elmer and Bronco responded to it. Bronco's eight legs went up and down like pistons gone berserk and between the pumping, dancing legs his body bobbed and swayed. The ground beneath their feet thundered like a drum and it seemed to me that I could feel the vibrations through my soles. The people yelled and whooped. Some of them standing outside the circle had began to dance and the others now joined in, dancing along with Bronco and with Elmer.

I looked to one side of me and the old man was dancing, too, jigging wildly up and down, with his white hair flying and his white beard flapping and jerking with the violence of his motion. "Dance!" he yelled at me, his breath short and rasping in his throat. "What's the matter, you ain't dancing?"

And as he said it he reached into his pocket and, hauling out the bottle, handed it to me. I reached out and grabbed it and began to dance. I pulled the cork out of the bottle and put it to my mouth while dancing and the glass of the bottle's neck rattled on my teeth and some of the liquor sprayed onto my face and a good, solid slug of it went down my throat. It hit my gut and lay there warm and sloshing, and I danced, waving the bottle high, and I think I did some yelling, not that there was anything to yell about, but for the pure joy of the night.

We were, all of us, pure and simple crazy—crazy with the night and fire and music. We danced without a thought or purpose. Each of us danced because all the others danced, or because two sleek machines were out there dancing, their basic awkwardness transformed to matchless grace, or perhaps we simply danced because we were alive and deep within us knew we would not always be alive.

The moon floated in the sky and the wood smoke from the fire trailed in a slender column of whiteness up into the sky. The screeching fiddles and the twanging guitars shrieked and sobbed and sang.

Suddenly, as if by command (although there was no command), the music stuttered to a halt and the dancing stopped. I saw the others stop and stopped myself, with the bottle still held high.

I felt someone pawing at my lifted arm and a voice said, "The bottle, man. For pity's sake, the bottle."

It was the old man. I gave him the bottle. He used it as a pointer to indicate one side of the circle and then he tucked its neck into his whiskers and tilted back his head. The bottle gurgled and his Adam's apple jerked in concert with the gurgling.

Looking where he'd pointed, I saw a man standing quietly there. He wore a black robe of some sort that came down to his feet and that had a cowl on it, covering his head, so that all that showed of him was the white smear of his face.

The old man sputtered, half strangled, and took the bottle from his face. He used it to point again.

"The census-taker," he said.

The people were drawing back and away from the census-taker, and on the platform the musicians sat limp, mopping their faces with their shirt sleeves.

The census-taker stood there for a moment, with all the people gaping at him, then he floated—he didn't walk, he floated—to the center of the dancing circle. The man with the reed instrument lifted it to his lips and began a piping that at first was the sound of the wind moving through the grasses of a meadow, then grew louder, trilling a string of notes that one could almost see hanging in the air. The violins came in softly as a background to the piping and as if from some distant place the guitars twanged a hollow sound and then the violins sobbed and the piping went insane and the guitars were humming like vibratory drums.

Out in the circle, the census-taker was dancing, not with his feet—you couldn't see his feet because of the robe he wore—but with his body swaying like a dish cloth hanging on a line and whipping in the wind, a strange, distorted, dangling dance such as a puppet would perform.

He was not alone. There were others with him, many shadowy shapes that had come from nowhere and were dancing with him, the firelight shining through the unsubstantial shimmer of their ghostly bodies. They were simply shapes at first, but as I stared at them, astonished, they began to take on more definite form and feature, although they did not gain in substantiality. They still were nebulous and hazy, but now they were people rather than just shapes, and I saw with horror that they wore the costumes of many different races from far among the stars. There a bewhiskered brigand in the kilt and cape of that distant planet that was called, curiously enough, End of Nothing; there the jolly merchant with his stately toga from the planet Cash, and between them, dancing with abandon in a tattered gown, a rope of gems about her neck, a girl who could have been from nowhere else but the pleasure planet Vegas.

She didn't touch me and I didn't hear her come, but with some sense I did not know I had, I became aware that Cynthia was beside me. I looked down at her and she was staring up at me, with mingled fear and wonder on her face. Her lips moved, but I couldn't hear her because of the loudness of the music.

"What did you say?" I asked, but she had no time to answer, for in the instant that I spoke, a concussion slapped me over and I went down on the ground so hard that the breath was knocked out of me. I landed on my side and rolled over on my back and I saw, with some surprise, Bronco flying through the air, with all eight legs spraddled out grotesquely, while all around burning logs and brands were flying and a puff of smoke floated up to dim the brilliance of the moon.

I tried to breathe and couldn't and a sudden panic hit me—that I'd never breathe again, that I was done with breathing. Then I did breathe, taking in great gulps of air, and each gulp was so agonizing that I tried to stop, but couldn't.

All over the clearing, I saw, people had been thrown to the ground. Some of them were getting up and others were trying to get up and there were many others who were just lying there.

I struggled to my knees and saw that Cynthia, beside me,

was also trying to get up and I put out a hand to help her. Bronco was sprawled out on the ground and as I watched, he finally gained his feet, but two of his legs, both on the same side, dangled, and he stood there unsteadily on the other six.

A thunder of feet went past me and Elmer was at Bronco's side, holding him erect, propping him, helping him to move. I got to my feet and pulled Cynthia up beside me. Elmer and Bronco were coming toward us and Elmer yelled at us, "Get out of here! Up across the hill!"

We turned and ran, coming to the fence on which the old man, Henry, and myself had squatted half the afternoon. And coming to it, I knew that the crippled Bronco could never make his way across it. I grabbed a post with both my hands and tried to pull it loose and force it down. It wiggled back and forth, but I could not topple it.

"Let me," said Elmer, close beside me. He lifted a foot and kicked and the boards splintered and came loose. Cynthia had crawled through the fence and was running up the hill. I ran after her.

I took one quick look behind me as I ran and saw that one of the haystacks close beside the barn was burning, set afire, most likely, by one of the flaming brands sent flying through the air by the explosion that had crippled Bronco. People were running aimlessly in the light of the burning stack.

Looking back, not watching where I was going, I ran into a cornshock and, toppling it, went down on top of it.

By the time I disentangled myself and was on my feet again, Elmer and Bronco had gone on past me and were disappearing over the brow of the moonlit hill. I sprinted after them. My face and hands smarted and burned from their forcible contact with the sun-dried corn leaves and when I put my hand up to my face it came away wet and sticky with blood oozing from the cuts the dry, sharp leaves had inflicted on my skin.

I went plunging down the hill below the brow and far ahead of me saw the whiteness of Cynthia's jacket, almost at the woods that ran below the field. Not far behind her were Bronco and Elmer. Bronco had caught the hang of being helped along by Elmer and they were moving rapidly.

The stubs of the cut corn and the autumn-dried weeds that had grown between the rows rasped against my trousers as I ran and behind me I heard the shouts and bellows from the clearing beyond the field.

I reached the fence that ran between the field and woods and there was a gateway through it where Elmer had kicked the boards loose. I plunged through the opening and in among the trees, and here, while there still was moonlight shining through the branches, I had to slow my pace for fear of crashing headlong into one of the trees.

Someone hissed at me, off to one side, and I slowed and swung around. I saw that the three of them were grouped beneath an oak with low-growing branches. Bronco was braced on his six legs and doing fairly well. Elmer was climbing down out of the tree, dragging bundles with him.

"I brought them out here and cached them," he said, "shortly after dark. I had it in my mind something like this might happen."

"Do you know what happened?"

"Someone threw a bomb," said Elmer.

"Cemetery bomb," I said. "They had that case of booze."

"Payment," Elmer said.

"I suppose so. I had wondered. It was damn good whiskey."

"But what about the census-taker and the ghosts?" asked Cynthia. "If they were ghosts."

"Diversion," Elmer said.

I shook my head. "It gets too complicated. Everyone couldn't have been in on it."

"You underestimate our friends," said Elmer. "What did you say to Bell?"

"Not a great deal. I resisted being taken over."

Elmer grunted. "That's *lèse majesté*," he said.

"What do we do now?" asked Cynthia.

Elmer said to Bronco, "Can you manage for a while without me?"

"If I go slow," said Bronco.

"Fletch will be with you. He can't hold you up like I can, but if you should fall he can boost you up. With him helping, you can manage. I have to get some tools."

"You have your kit of tools," I said. And that was right. He had all those replacement hands and a lot of other things. They were stored in a compartment in his chest.

"I may need a hammer and some heavier stuff. Those legs of Bronco's are knocked all out of shape. It may take some hammering and refitting to get them back again. There's a tool house back there. It's locked, but that isn't any problem."

"I thought the idea was for us to get away. If you go back there . . ."

"They're all upset. That barn is about to go and they'll be fighting fire. I can slip in and out."

"You'll hurry," Cynthia said.

He nodded. "I'll hurry. The three of you go down this hill until you reach a valley, then turn to the right, downstream. You take this pack, Fletch, and Cynthia, you should be able to handle this smaller one. Leave the rest of it for me; I'll bring it along. Bronco can't carry anything, the shape that he is in."

"Just one thing," I said.

"What is that?"

"How do you know we should turn right, downstream?"

"Because I was out scouting while you were roosting on a fence with your bewhiskered pal and Cynthia was peeling potatoes and performing other housewifely chores. From years of experience I have learned it's always a good idea to scout out your ground."

"But where are we heading for?" asked Cynthia.

He told her, "Away from Cemetery. As far as we can get."

10

Bronco had said that he could manage, but it was slow going. The hillside was steep and rough and it was a long way down to the valley and Bronco fell three times before we reached the valley floor. Each time I managed to heave him up, but it took a lot of work and a lot of time.

Behind us, for a while, a brilliance waved and flickered in the sky and it must have been the barn, for a haystack would have burned out more quickly. But by the time we reached the valley the brilliance was gone. The barn either had burned down or the fire had been put out.

The traveling was easier in the valley. The ground was fairly level, although there were rough stretches here and there. There were fewer trees and the moon shed more light than it had on the heavily wooded hillside. Off to our left somewhere a stream was flowing. We did not come across it, but every now and then we could hear the chuckle of its water when apparently it flowed across a gravel bar.

We moved through an eerie world of silver magic and from the hills on either side came, at intervals, a far-off whickering and sometimes other sounds. Once a great bird came floating down above us, with not a whisper from its wings, veering to slide off above a clump of trees.

"If only," Bronco said, "I had got one leg damaged on either side, it would have caused no trouble, but this business of two legs on one side and four legs on the other is most confusing and makes me ridiculously lopsided."

"You are doing splendidly," said Cynthia. "Does it hurt?"

"I have no hurt," said Bronco. "I cannot have a hurt."

"You think Cemetery did it," Cynthia said to me. "And so does Elmer, and so, I would suppose, do I. But surely we can't pose a threat . . ."

"Anyone," I said, "who does not bow down to Cemetery is automatically a threat. They have been here so long, have held the Earth so long, that they cannot bear the slightest interference."

"But we are no interference."

"We could be. If we get back to Alden, if we get off Earth with what we came to get, we could interfere with them. We could present a picture of the Earth that is not Cemetery. And it just might catch on, it might gain some public and artistic recognition. The people might be pleased to think the Earth was not entirely Cemetery."

"Even so," she said, "it would hurt them in no way. They still could carry on their business. There would be really nothing changed."

"It would hurt their pride," I said.

"But pride is such a little thing to hurt—purely personal thing. Whose pride? The pride of Maxwell Peter Bell, the pride of other little autocrats the like of Maxwell Bell. Not the pride of Cemetery. Cemetery is a corporation, a massive corporation. It thinks in terms of income, in the annual business volume, in profits and in costs. There is no place in its ledgers for such a thing as pride. It must be something else, Fletch. It can't be entirely pride."

She could be right, I told myself. It could be something more than pride, but what?

"They are used to ruling," I said. "They can buy anything they want. They hired someone to throw that bomb at Bronco. Even when there was a chance that others would get hurt. Because they don't care, you see. Just so they get what they want, they do not really care. And they get things cheap. Because of who they are, no one can question what they offer. We know the price of that bomb and it was cheap enough. A case of whiskey. Maybe, if they are to keep an upper hand, they must demonstrate, very forcibly, what happens to those people who slip from beneath their thumb."

"You keep saying they," said Cynthia. "There is no they here, there is no Cemetery. There is only one man here."

"That is true," I said, "and that is why pride could be a factor. Not so much the pride of Cemetery as the pride of Maxwell Bell."

The valley spread before us, a broad road of grasses, broken by little clumps of trees and rimmed in by the dark and wooded hills. Off to the left was the stream, but it had been some time since we had heard any sound of it. The ground was level and Bronco was able to proceed without too much trouble, although it was painful to witness his awkward, hobbling gait. But even so, he was easily able to keep up with our human walking.

There was no sign of Elmer. I held my wrist close to my face and my watch said that it was almost two o'clock. I had no idea when we had left the clearing, but thinking back on it, it seemed to me that it could not have been much later than ten, which meant we'd been four hours on the road. I wondered if something might have happened to Elmer. It would not have taken him much time to break into the tool house and get whatever he might need. He would have had to pick up the packs we'd left behind and he'd be hauling quite a load, but even so, the weight should not slow him too much and he'd still travel fairly fast.

If he didn't show up by daylight, I decided, we'd have to find some place where we could hole up and keep a watch for him. Neither Cynthia nor myself had had any sleep to speak of since we'd reached the Earth and I was beginning to feel it and I supposed that she was, too. Bronco didn't need to sleep. He could keep a watch for Elmer while we did some sleeping.

"Fletcher," Cynthia said. She had stopped just ahead of me and I bumped into her. Bronco skidded to a halt.

"Smoke," she said. "I smell smoke. Wood smoke."

I smelled no smoke.

"You're imagining it," I said. "There is no one here."

92

The valley didn't have the feel of people. It had the feel of moonlight and grass and trees and hills, of light and shadow, night air and flying things. Back in the hills there was the whickering every now and then and other night-time noises, but there were no people, no sense or feel of people.

Then I smelled the smoke, the faintest whiff of it, an acrid tang in the air, there one moment, gone the next.

"You're right," I said. "There is a fire somewhere."

"Fire means people," Bronco said.

"I've had my belly full of people," Cynthia said. "I don't want to see anyone for another day or two."

"Me either," Bronco said.

We stood there, waiting for another whiff of smoke, but it did not come.

"There might be no one around," I said. "A tree struck by lightning days ago and still burning. An old camp fire that no one bothered to put out, still smoldering."

"We should get under cover," Cynthia said, "not stay standing out here where anyone can see us."

"There is a grove over to the left," said Bronco. "We could get there rather rapidly."

We turned toward the left, heading for the grove, moving slowly and cautiously. And I thought how silly it all would seem when daylight came, for the fire that produced the smoke could be several miles away. Probably there was no reason to be fearful of it, even so. Provided they were there, whoever had built that fire might be very decent people.

Almost at the grove we stopped to listen and from the direction of the grove came the sound of running water. That was good, I thought. I was getting thirsty. The trees more than likely grew along the stream that ran down through the valley.

We moved in among the trees, half-blinded by the denseness of the shadows underneath them after the bright moonlight in the open and as we moved into the shadows some of them rose up and clubbed me to the ground.

11

I had fallen into a lake somehow and was sinking for the third and final time, strangling, with water on my face and water up my nose and no way I could breathe. I gagged and gasped and opened up my eyes and water streaming from my hair ran down across my face.

I saw that I was not in any lake, but rather on dry land, and in the light of a fire that burned a little ways away I could see the dark figure of a man who held a wooden bucket in both hands and I knew that he had thrown a bucket full of water in my face.

I couldn't see his face too well, with his back turned to the firelight, but he flashed a set of white teeth at me, yelling something in an angry voice I did not understand.

There was a terrible ruckus going on off to my right and when I turned my head in that direction I saw that it was Bronco, flat on his back, with a lot of yelling men around him, dodging in and out, trying to get at him. But they weren't getting at him too well, for even with two busted legs, Bronco had six that weren't busted and all six of them were busily lashing out at the men around him.

I looked around for Cynthia and saw her by the fire. She was sitting rather awkwardly on the ground and one arm was lifted strangely and I saw that a big man who stood beside her had the raised arm in his grasp and when she tried to get to her feet he twisted it and she sat down again, rather solidly.

I started to get up and as I did the man with the bucket rushed me, swinging the bucket as if he meant to brain me.

94

I didn't get clear up, but did manage to get my feet in under me and was in a crouch and when I saw the bucket coming at me, shifted to one side and stretched out an arm. The bucket barely missed me and then, as he came charging in, I had him by the legs. As he fell toward me, I hunched down one shoulder and caught him at the knees and he went catapulting over me to land with a crash behind me. I didn't wait to see what had happened to him or what he might be doing, but launched myself across the few feet that separated us at the man who had Cynthia by the arm.

He saw me coming and let go of her arm and clawed at his belt for a knife, but he was slow in getting it and I let him have it squarely on the chin, bringing my fist up from somewhere near my boot tops. I swear the blow lifted him a full foot off the ground and his body, stiff as any pole, went toppling backward. He hit the ground and lay there and I reached down and grabbed Cynthia to help her to her feet, although I suspect she had no need of aid.

Even as I helped her to her feet there was a bellowing behind me and as I swung around to face it I saw that the men who had been ganging up on Bronco had left him and were moving in on me.

From that moment when the bucket of water had struck me in the face and revived me from the blow upon the head, I had been too busy to take in much of the detail of the situation we were in, but now I had the time to notice that the men who were advancing upon me were an unsavory lot. Some of them were dressed in what I supposed were buckskins and some of them wore fur caps upon their heads and even in the feeble firelight I could see they were a ragged and a dirty lot and that they moved in slouching crouches, not upright and forthright as a man should walk. Some of them carried guns of some sort, and here and there there were flashes of metal from drawn knives and, all in all, I decided, I did not have much chance to stand against them.

"You better get out of here," I said to Cynthia. "Try to find a place to hide."

There was no answer from her and when I looked around to see why she had not answered, I saw that she was stooping and groping on the ground. She rose from her stoop and in each hand she clutched a club, awkward lengths of tree limbs that she had snatched off a pile of fuel that apparently had been hauled in to feed the fire. She thrust one out at me and, with a two-handed grip upon the other, ranged herself beside me.

So we stood there, the two of us, with the clubs clutched in our hands, and it might have been a brave gesture of a sort, but I knew how ineffectual it would be.

The group of men had stopped at the sight of us suddenly armed with clubs, but any time they wanted, they could close in and get us. Some few of them, perhaps, would take their lumps, but they'd overwhelm us by sheer numbers.

A big brute, who stood slightly in the front, said, "What's the matter with you two? Why you got the clubs?"

"You jumped us," I said.

"You sneaked up on us," said the man.

"We smelled the smoke," said Cynthia. "We were not sneaking up."

Somewhere off to the left there were snorting noises and the sound of feet or hooves tramping on the ground. There were animals somewhere in the grove of trees beyond the fire.

"You were sneaking," the man insisted. "You and that great beast of yours."

While he talked others in the group were shifting off to either side. They were getting in position to take us from the flanks.

"Let us talk some sense," I said. "We are travelers. We didn't know that you were here and . . ."

There was a sudden rush of feet from either side of us and from somewhere in the woods rang out a ululating cry that stopped the sudden rush—a wild and savage war cry that froze the blood in one and made the hair stand up. Out of the screen of woods broke a towering metal figure, mov-

96

ing very fast, and at the sight of it the pack that had been about to swarm in on us were running for their lives.

"Elmer!" Cynthia shrieked, but he paid no attention to us. One of the fleeing men had stumbled when he had set out to run and Elmer snapped him up in the middle of his stride, lifted his twisting, frantic body high into the air and threw him out into the darkness. A gun exploded and there was a hollow thud as the ball hit Elmer's metal body, but that was the only shot the fleeing men took the time to fire. They went crashing into the woods beyond the fire, with Elmer close upon their heels. They were yelling out in fright and between the yells one could hear the splashing as they fought their way across the stream that lay beyond the campsite.

Cynthia was running toward the struggling Bronco, and I ran after her. Between the two of us, we got him on his feet.

"That was Elmer," Bronco said, once we got him up. "He will give them hell."

The cries and whoops were receding in the distance. "There be more of them," said Bronco, "tethered in the woods. They have no ill in them, however, for they are but simple creatures."

"Horses," said Cynthia. "There must be quite a lot of them. I think these people must be traders."

"Can you tell me exactly what went on?" I asked her. "We were just entering the woods and there were some shadows. Then I came to with someone throwing water in my face."

"They hit you," Cynthia said, "and grabbed me and dragged us to the fire. They dragged you by the heels and you were a funny sight."

"I imagine you died laughing."

"No," she said, "I wasn't laughing, but you still were funny."

"And Bronco?"

"I was galloping to your rescue," Bronco said, "when I tripped and fell. And there, upon my back, I gave a good account of myself, would you not say so? As they clustered all about me, I got in some lusty licks with my trusty hooves."

"There was no sign of them," said Cynthia. "They lay in wait for us. They saw us coming and they laid in wait for us. We couldn't see the fire, for it was in a fairly deep ravine . . ."

"They had sentries out, of course," I said. "It was just our luck that we fell foul of them."

We moved down to the fire and stood around it. It had fairly well died down, but we did not stir it up. Somehow we felt just a little safer if there were not too much light. Boxes and bales were piled to one side of it and on the other side a pile of wood that had been dragged in as fuel. Cooking and eating utensils, guns and blankets lay scattered all about.

Something splashed very noisely across the stream and came crashing through the brush. I made a dive to grab up a gun, but Bronco said, "It's only Elmer coming back," and I dropped the gun. I don't know why I picked it up; I had not the least idea of how it might have worked.

Elmer came crunching through the brush.

"They got away," he said. "I tried to catch one of them to hear what he might have to say, but they were too nimble for me."

"They were scared," said Bronco.

"Is everyone all right?" asked Elmer. "How about you, miss?"

"We're all right," said Cynthia. "One of them hit Fletcher with a club and knocked him out, but he seems to be all right."

"I have a lump," I said, "and my head, come to think of it, seems a little sore. But there's nothing wrong with me."

"Fletch," said Elmer, "why don't you build up the fire and get some food to cooking. You and Miss Cynthia must feel some need of it. Some sleep, too, perhaps. I dropped the stuff I was carrying. I'll go back and get it."

"Hadn't we ought to be getting out of here?" I asked.

"They won't be coming back," said Elmer. "Not right now. Not in broad daylight and dawn's about to break. They'll come back tomorrow night, but we'll be gone by then."

"They have some animals tied out in the woods," said Bronco. "Pack animals, no doubt, to carry those bales and boxes. We could use some animals such as that."

"We'll take them along," said Elmer. "We'll leave our friends afoot. And another thing—I'm most anxious to look into those bales. There must be something in them they didn't want to have anybody poking into."

"Maybe not," said Bronco. "Maybe they were just spoiling for a fight. Maybe they were just mean and ornery."

12

But it wasn't just meanness.

They had reason to want no one knowing what was in the bales and boxes.

The first bale, when we ripped it open, contained metal, crudely cut into plates, apparently with chisels.

Elmer picked up two of the plates and banged them together, "Steel," he said, "plated with bronze. I wonder where they'd get stuff like this."

But even before he got through saying it, he knew, and so did I. He looked at me and saw I knew, or guessed, and said, "It's casket metal, Fletch."

We stood around and looked at it, with Bronco back of us, looking over our shoulders. Elmer dropped the two pieces he'd been holding.

"I'll go back and get the tools," he said, "and we'll get to work on Bronco. We have to get out of here sooner than I thought."

We got to work, using the tools that Elmer had taken from the tool shack back at the settlement. One leg we fixed up with little effort, straightening it and hammering it out and slipping it back into place so that it worked as good as new. The second leg gave us some trouble.

"How long do you think this might have been going on?" I asked as we worked. "This robbing of the Cemetery. Certainly Cemetery must know about it."

"Perhaps they do," said Elmer, "but what can they do about it and why should they care? If someone wants to do some genteel grave-robbing, what difference does it make? Just so they do it where it doesn't show too much."

"But they would surely notice. They keep the Cemetery trimmed and . . ."

"Where it can be seen," said Elmer. "I'll lay you a bet there are places where there is no care at all—places that visitors never are allowed to see."

"But if someone comes to visit a certain grave?"

"They'd know about it ahead of time. They'd know the names on any Pilgrim passenger list—the names and where the passengers were from. They'd have time to put on a crash program, getting any sector of the Cemetery cleaned up. Or maybe they wouldn't even have to. Maybe they'd simply switch a few headstones or markers and who would know the difference?"

Cynthia had been cooking at the fire. Now she came over to us. "Could I use this for a minute?" she asked, picking up a pinch bar.

"Sure, we're through with it," said Elmer. "We've almost got old Bronco here as good as new. What do you want with it?"

"I thought I'd open up one of the boxes."

"No need to," Elmer said. "We know what they were carrying. It'll just be more metal."

"I don't care," said Cynthia. "I would like to see."

It was growing light. The sun was brightening the eastern sky and would soon be rising. Birds, which had begun their twittering as soon as the darkness of the night had started to fade, now were flying and hopping in the trees. One bird, big and blue and with a topknot, moved nervously about, screeching at us.

"A blue jay," Elmer said. "Noisy kind of creatures. Remember them of old. Some of the others, too, but not all their names. That one is a robin. Over there a blackbird—a redwing blackbird, I would guess. Cheeky little rascal."

"Fletcher," Cynthia said, not speaking very loudly, but her voice sharp and strained.

I had been squatting, watching Elmer put the last

101

touches to straightening out and shaping one of Bronco's hooves.

"Yes," I said, "what is it?" not even looking around.

"Please come here," she said.

I rose and turned around. She had managed to lift one end of a board off the top of a box and had pushed it up and left it, canted at an angle. She wasn't looking toward me. She was looking at what the lifting of the board had revealed inside the box, unmoving, as if she had been suddenly hypnotized, unable to take her eyes away from what she saw inside the box.

The sight of her standing in this fashion brought me suddenly alert and in three quick strides, I was beside her.

The first thing that I saw was the exquisitely decorated bottle—tiny, dainty, of what appeared to be jade, but it could not have been jade, for there was painted on it small, delicate figures in black and yellow and dark green, while the bottle itself was an apple green—and nothing in its right mind would go about painting jade. It lay against a china cup, or what appeared to be a china cup, emblazoned in red and blue, and beside the cup a grotesque piece of statuary, rudely carved out of cream-colored stone. Lying half hidden by the statuary was a weirdly decorated jar.

Elmer had come up to us and now he reached out and took the pinch bar away from Cynthia. In two quick motions, he ripped the rest of the boards away. The box was filled with a jumble of jars and bottles, bits of statuary, pieces of china, cunningly shaped bits of metalwork, begemmed belts and bracelets, necklaces of stone, brooches, symbolic pieces (they must have been symbolic pieces, for they made no other sense), boxes of both wood and metal, and many other items.

I picked up one of the symbolic pieces, a many-sided block of some sort of polished stone, with half-obscured etchings on every face of it. I turned it in my hand, looking closely at the engraved symbols presented on each face. It was heavy, as if it might be of metal rather than of stone, although it seemed to have a rocklike texture. I could almost remember, almost be sure, although absolute certainty escaped me. There had been a similar piece, a very similar piece, on the mantel in Thorney's study, and one night while we had sat there he had taken it up and showed me how it had been used, rolled like a die to decide a course of action to be taken, a divining stone of some sort and very, very ancient and extremely valuable and significant because it was one of the few artifacts that could unmistakably be attributed to a most obscure people on a far-off, obscure planet—a people who had lived there and died or moved away or evolved into something else long before the human race had found the planet vacant and had settled down on it.

"You know what it is, Fletch?" Elmer asked.

"I'm not sure," I said. "Thorney had one that was almost like it. A very ancient piece. He named the planet and the people, but I can't recall the names. He was always telling me the planet and the people."

"The food is hot," said Cynthia. "Why don't we eat it now? We can talk about it while we eat."

I realized, when she spoke of it, that I was ravenous. I had not tasted food since the noon before.

She led the way to the fire and dished up the food from the pan in which she'd heated it. It was a thick, rich soup, almost a stew, with vegetables and chunks of meat in it. In my haste, I burned my mouth with the first spoonful.

Elmer squatted down beside us. He picked up a stick and idly poked the fire.

"It seems to me," he said, "that we have here some of those missing items that you told me Professor Thorndyke often talked about. Stuff from archaeological sites looted by treasure hunters who spirited all their findings away so they could not be studied, probably to be sold at a later time, at tremendous profit, to collectors."

"I think you are right," I said, "and now I think I know where at least some of them are hidden out."

"In the Cemetery," Cynthia said.

"Nothing would be simpler," I said. "A casket would make an excellent hiding place. No one would think of digging it up—no one, that is, other than a gang of outland metal seekers who figured out where they could get good metal at no more than the cost of a little work."

"It would have been the metal at first," said Cynthia, "and then one day they found a casket that held no body, but was filled with treasure. Maybe there was a way in which the graves that held the treasure would be marked. Perhaps a simple little design you would never see unless you knew where to look on the tombstone or the marker."

"They wouldn't have found that mark to start with," said Elmer. "It might have taken them quite a while to get it figured out."

"They probably had a long time to get it figured out," said Cynthia. "These ghouls of ours may have been at this metal business for hundreds of years."

"There may have been no mark," I said.

"Why, there must have been," said Cynthia. "How else would they know where to dig?"

"How about someone in the Cemetery working with them? Some insider who would know which graves to dig?"

"You are both forgetting something," Elmer said. "Maybe our ghoulish friends aren't really interested in those trinkets in the boxes . . ."

"But they took them," Cynthia said.

"Sure, they'd take them. They may be interesting and amusing. They might even have some trade value. But it seems to me it is the metal they really would be after. Metal, after all these years, would be hard to come by. At first it could be picked up in the cities, but after a time much of the cities-metal would be badly corroded and you'd have to mine for it. But in the Cemetery there is more recent metal, perhaps much better metal. The artifacts they find in some of the graves have value for us because we have been told by Professor Thorndyke they are significant, but I doubt they have value for these robbers. Toys for the children, geegaws for the women, perhaps minor trading stock—but it's the metal they are after."

"This business explains one thing," I said. "It sheds some light on why Cemetery wants to keep control of visitors. They wouldn't want to take a chance of someone finding out about the artifacts."

"It's not illegal," Cynthia said.

"No, of course it's not. The archaeologists have tried for years to get legislation halting the trade in artifacts, but they've been unable to."

"It's sneaky, though," said Elmer, "and unprincipled. It's an underhanded business. If it should leak out, it might do much to tarnish Cemetery's shiny reputation."

"But they let us go," said Cynthia.

"There wasn't much at the moment they could have done about it," I said. "There was no way they could stop us."

"They did something later," said Elmer. "They tried to blow up Bronco."

Cynthia said, "If they'd destroyed Bronco, they figured we would get discouraged . . ."

"I think that is right," I said. "Although we can't be absolutely sure about the bomb."

"We can be fairly sure," said Elmer.

"There's one thing about it I don't like," I said. "Without half trying, we've managed to make enemies of everyone we've met. There is Cemetery and now this band of ghouls, and I would suppose the people back at the settlement do not think too kindly of us. Because of us they lost some haystacks and a barn and maybe some of them may have been hurt and . . ."

"They brought it on themselves," said Elmer.

"That won't stop them blaming us."

"I suppose it won't," said Elmer.

"I think we should get out of here," I said.

"You and Miss Cynthia need some sleep."

I looked across the fire at her. "We can stay awake for a few hours more," I said.

She nodded bleakly at me.

"We'll take along the horses," Elmer said. "That will slow them up. We can get their stuff loaded up . . ."

"Why bother with it," I said. "Leave it here. It does us no good. What could we do with it?"

"Why, sure," said Elmer. "Why couldn't I have thought of that? When they come back they'll have to leave some men to guard it and that splits up their force."

"They'll follow us," said Cynthia. "They have to have those horses."

"Sure they will," said Elmer, "and when they finally find the horses, if they ever do, we'll be miles away and out of reach."

Bronco spoke, for the first time. "But the human two. They cannot go minus sleep. They cannot go for hours."

"We'll figure something out," said Elmer. "Let's get going."

"About the census-taker and the ghosts?" asked Cynthia, asking, so far as I could see, without any reason.

"Let's not worry about the ghosts," I said.

She'd asked the same question once before. It was just like a woman. Get into some sort of trouble and they'll come up with the silly questions.

13

I woke and it was night, but immediately I remembered what had happened and where we were. I raised up to a sitting position and to one side of me saw the dark form that was Cynthia. She was still asleep. Just a few hours more, I thought, and Elmer and Bronco would be back and we could be on our way. It had been all damn foolishness, I told myself. We could have kept on with them. I had been sleepy, certainly, and riding a horse for the first time in my life had not been an easy chore, but I could have managed. Cynthia had been played out, but we could have strapped her onto Bronco so that if she fell asleep she would not have fallen off, but Elmer had insisted on leaving us behind while he and Bronco shagged the horses deep into the mountains that loomed ahead of us.

"There can't nothing happen," he had said. "This cave is comfortable and well hidden and by the time you've had some sack time we'll be back again. There is nothing to it."

I blamed myself. I should not have let him talk us into it. I didn't like it, I told myself. We should have stayed together. No matter what had happened, we should have stayed together.

A shadow stirred near the mouth of the cave and a soft voice said, "Friend, please do not make an outcry. There is nothing you must fear."

I came surging to my feet, the hair prickling at the nape of my neck. "Who the hell are you?" I shouted.

"Softly, softly, softly," said the voice, softly. "There are those who must not hear."

Cynthia screamed.

"Shut up!" I yelled at her.

"You must be quiet," said the lurker in the shadows. "You do not recognize me, but I saw you at the dance."

Cynthia, on the verge of another scream, caught her breath and gulped. "It's the census-taker," she said. "What does he want here?"

"I come, fair one," said the census-taker, "to warn you of great danger."

"You would," I said, but I did not say it loudly, for all this business of his about talking softly and not making any outcry had sunken into me.

"The wolves," he said. "The metal wolves have been set upon your trail."

"What can we do about it?"

"You stay very quiet," said the census-taker, "and hope that they pass by."

"Where are all your pals?" I asked.

"They are around somewhere. They are often with me. They hide when they first meet people. They are a little shy. If they like you they'll come out."

"They weren't shy at the dance the other night," said Cynthia.

"They were among old friends. They had been there before."

"You said something about wolves," I reminded him. "Metal wolves, I think."

"If you'll come most softly to the entrance, I think that you might see them. But please to be most quiet."

Cynthia was close beside me and I put out my hand to her and she grabbed it and hung on tight.

"Metal wolves," she said.

"Robots, more than likely." I don't know why I was so calm about it. Stupidity, I guess. In the last two days we had encountered so many screwy things that metal wolves, at first, didn't seem too bad. Just sort of commonplace.

Outside the cave mouth the moon lighted up the landscape. The trees stood out almost as plain as if it had been day and in between them ran little grassy places dotted with boulders. It was wild, rough country and, somehow, it sent a shiver through me.

We crouched just inside the entrance and there was not a thing to see, just the trees and the grassy patches and the boulders and beyond them the dark lift of hills fearsome in their darkness.

"I don't . . ." Cynthia began, but the census-taker clucked at her and she said no more.

We crouched, the two of us, hand in hand, and it seemed a silly business. There was nothing stirring; not even the trees, for there was no wind.

Then there was a movement in the shadow underneath a tree and a moment later the thing that had made the movement trotted out into the open. It glittered in the moonlight and it had about it a sense of fiendish strength and ferocity. It was the size of a calf, perhaps, although because of the moonlight and the distance, the size was hard to judge. It was lithe and quick, with a nervousness about it, stepping high and daintily, but there was in its metal body a feel of power that could be perceived even from some hundreds of feet away. It quartered nervously about, as if it might be seeking out a scent and for a moment it switched about and stared directly at us—stared and seemed to strain toward us, as if someone might have held it on a leash and it yearned to break away.

Then it turned and took up its running back and forth and all at once there were three instead of one of them—slipping through the moonlight, running in the woods.

One of them, as it turned toward us in its running, opened its mouth, or what would have been its mouth had it been a biologic creature, exposing a seried rank of metal teeth. When it shut its mouth, the clash of the teeth coming back together came clear to us, crouching in the cave.

Cynthia was pressing close against me and I disengaged my hand from hers, put my arm about her and held her very close, not thinking of her, I am sure, as a woman in that moment, but as another human being, another thing of flesh and blood that metal teeth could rend. Clutching one another, we watched the wolves, seeking, running—I got the impression they were slavering—and, somehow the idea crept into my mind that they knew we were nearby and were seeking us.

Then they were gone. As quickly as they had appeared, they disappeared, and we did not see them go. But we still stayed crouching there, afraid to speak, afraid to move. How long we stayed, I do not know.

Then fingers tapped against my shoulder. "They are gone," the census-taker said. I had, until he tapped me, forgotten about the census-taker.

"They were confused," he said. "Undoubtedly the horses milled around down there while you were being installed in the cave before your companions went away. It took them a while to work out the trail."

Cynthia tried to speak and choked, the words dying in her throat. I knew exactly how it was; my own mouth was so dry I wondered if I would ever speak again.

She tried again and made it. "I thought they were looking for us. I thought they knew we were somewhere near."

"It is over now," the census-taker said. "The present danger's past. Why don't we move back into the cave and be comfortable?"

I rose, dragging Cynthia up with me. My muscles were tense and knotted from staying still so long in such an uncomfortable position. After staring so long out into the moonlight, the cave was dark as pitch, but I groped along the wall, found our piles of sacks and baggage and, sitting down, leaned against them. Cynthia sat down beside me.

The census-taker squatted down in front of us. We couldn't really see him because the robe he wore was as black as the inside of the cave. All one could see of him was the whiteness of his face, a pasty blob in the darkness, a blob without any features.

"I suppose," I said, "that we should thank you."

He made a shrugging motion. "One seldom comes on

allies," he said. "When one does he makes the most of it, does whatever is possible to do."

There were moving shadows in the cave, flickering shadows. Either they had just arrived or I had failed to notice them before. Now they were everywhere.

"Have you called in your people?" Cynthia asked, and from the tightness of her voice I guessed what it must have cost to keep it level.

"They have been here all the time," said the census-taker. "It takes them a little to show themselves. They come on slow and easy. They have no wish to frighten."

"It is difficult," said Cynthia, "not to be frightened by ghosts. Or do you call them something else?"

"A better term," said the census-taker, "might be shades."

"Why shades?" I asked.

"The reason," said the census-taker, "is one of somewhat involved semantics that would require an evening to explain. I am not sure I entirely understand myself. But it is the term they do prefer."

"And you?" I asked. "Exactly what are you?"

"I do not understand," said the census-taker.

"Look, we are humans. These other folks are shades. The creatures we were watching were robots—metal wolves. A matter of classification. How are you classified?"

"Oh, that," said the census-taker. "That really is quite simple. I am a census-taker."

"And the wolves," said Cynthia. "I suppose they are Cemetery."

"Oh, yes, indeed," said the census-taker, "although now only rarely used. In the early days there was much work for them to do."

I was puzzled. "What kind of work?" I asked.

"Monsters," said the census-taker and I could see that he did not want to talk about it.

The shades had stopped their incessant fluttering and were beginning to settle down so that one could see or at least guess at the shape of them.

"They like you," said the census-taker. "They know you're on their side."

"We're not on anyone's side," I told him. "We're just running like hell to keep from getting clipped. Ever since we arrived there has been someone taking potshots at us."

One of the shades had squatted down beside the census-taker, shedding, as it did so, some of its nebulous, misty quality and becoming not solid by any means, but a little more solid. One still had a sense of being able to see through them, but the swirly lines had stilled and the outlines were sharper, and this squatting thing looked something like a rather arty drawing made upon a blackboard with a piece of chalk.

"If you do not mind," said the arty piece of drawing, "I will introduce myself. My name was one that in the days long since struck terror on the planet Prairie, which is a strange name for a planet, but easily explained, because it is a very great planet, somewhat larger than the Earth and with land masses that are considerably larger than the areas of the oceans and all that land is flat, with no mountain, and all the land is prairie. There is no winter since the winds blow wild and free and the heat from the planet's sun is equitably distributed over the entire planetary surface. We settlers of Prairie lived in an eternal summer. We were, of course, humans from the planet Earth, our forebears landing on Prairie in their third migration outward into the galaxy, hopping from one planet to another in an attempt to find better living space, and on Prairie we found it—but perhaps not the way you think. We built no great cities, for reasons which I may explain later, but not now, since it would take too long to tell. Rather, we became roaming nomads with our flocks and herds, which is, perhaps a more satisfactory way of life than any other man has been able to devise. There dwelt upon this planet a native population of most slimy, most ferocious and sneaky devils that refused to cooperate in any way with us and which did their best, in various nefarious ways, to do away with us. I started out, I think, to introduce myself, then forgot to tell

112

my name. It is a good Earth name, for my family and my clan were always very careful to keep alive the heritage of Earth and—"

"His name," said the census-taker, interrupting, "is Ramsay O'Gillicuddy, which is, in all conscience, a good Earth name. I tell it to you because, if left to him, he'd never manage to get around to it."

"And now," said the shade of Ramsay O'Gillicuddy, "since I have been introduced, I'll tell you the story of my life."

"No, you won't," said the census-taker. "We haven't got the time. There is much we must discuss."

"Then the story of my death."

"All right," the census-taker said, "if you keep it short."

"They caught me," said Ramsay O'Gillicuddy's shade, "and made me a captive, these slimy, greasy natives. I shall not detail the situation which led to this shameful thing, for it would require the explanation of certain circumstances which the census-taker infers there is not the time to tell. But they caught me, anyhow, and then they held a long deliberate discussion, within my hearing, which I did not at all enjoy, about how best to dispose of me. None of the suggested procedures calculated to bring about my demise were pretty for the prospective victim to hold in contemplation. Nothing simple, you understand, such as a blow upon the head or a cutting of the throat, but all rather long, drawn-out, and intricate operations. Finally, after hours of talking back and forth, during which they politely invited my personal reactions to each plan put forward, they decided upon skinning me alive, explaining that they would not really be killing me and that because of this I should bear them no ill-will and that if I could manage to survive without my skin they would be glad to let me go. Once they had my skin, they informed me, they intended tanning it to make a drum upon which they could beat out a message of mockery to my clan."

"With all due respect," I said, "with a lady present . . ." but he paid no attention to me. "After I was dead," he said, "and my body had been found, my clan decided to do a thing that had never been done before. All our honored dead had been buried on the prairie, with the graves unmarked, in the thought that a man could ask no more than to become one with the world that he had trod. Word had come to us some years ago of the Cemetery here on Earth, but we had paid slight attention to it because it was not our way. But now the clan met in council and decided that I should be accorded the honor of sleeping in the soil of Mother Earth. So a large barrel was made to house my poor remains which, pickled in alcohol, were carted to the planet's one poor spaceport where the barrel was stored for many months, awaiting the arrival of a ship, on which it was finally taken to the nearest port where a funeral ship made regular calls."

"You cannot comprehend," said the census-taker, "what this decision cost his clan. They are poor people on the planet Prairie and their only wealth is counted in their flocks and herds. It took them many years to build back the livestock that was required for Cemetery to perform its services. It was a noble sacrifice and it's a pity that it came out so sadly. Ramsay, as you may guess, was and still is the only inhabitant of Prairie ever to be buried in Cemetery—not that he was really buried there, not, at least, in quite the manner that had been intended. The officials of Cemetery, not the present management, but one of many years ago, happened at that time to need an extra casket to hide away certain items . . ."

"You mean artifacts," I said.

"You know of this?" asked the census-taker.

"We suspected it," I said.

"Your suspicions are quite right," said the census-taker, "and our poor friend here was one of the victims of their treachery and greed. His casket was used for artifacts and what was left of him was thrown into a deep gorge, a natural charnel pit, at the Cemetery's edge, and ever since that day his shade has wandered the Earth, as do so many others and for the self-same reason."

114

"You tell it well," said O'Gillicuddy, "and in very simple truth."

"But let us not, please," said Cynthia, "have any more of this. You have us quite convinced."

"We have not the time for more," said the census-taker. "We now must deliberate upon what further action the two of you should take. For once the wolves catch up with your two good friends, they will realize immediately that you are not with them and since Cemetery cares nothing about the two robots, but only for yourselves . . ."

"They'll come back for us," said Cynthia, sounding scared.

I wasn't too brave about it, either. I did not like the thought of those great metal brutes snapping at our heels.

"How do they follow?" I asked.

"They have a sense of smell," said the census-taker. "Not the same kind you humans have, but the ability to pick up and recognize the chemicals of odors. They have sharp sight. They might have trouble if you kept to high and stony ground, where you'd leave little trace and the scent of your passing would not cling. I had feared they might catch the scent of you when they came by a while ago, but you were higher than they were and a kindly up-draft of air must have carried the smell away from them."

"They will be following the horses," I said. "The trail will be wide open. They'll travel fast. It may be only a few hours from now they'll find we're not with the others."

"You'll have a little time," said the census-taker. "It's a few hours yet till dawn and you can't start until it's light. You'll have to travel fast and you can carry little with you."

"We'll take food," said Cynthia, "And blankets . . ."

"Not too much food," said the census-taker. "Only what you must. You'll find food along the way. You have fish hooks, have you not?"

"Yes, we have a few fish hooks," said Cynthia. "I bought a box of them, almost as an afterthought. But we can't live on fish."

"There are roots and berries."

"But we don't know which roots and berries."

"You do not need to know," said the census-taker. "I know all of them."

"You'll be going with us?"

"We'll be going with you," said the census-taker.

"Of course we will," said O'Gillicuddy. "Every one of us. It's little we can do, but we'll be of some slight service. We can watch for followers . . ."

"But ghosts . . ." I said.

"Shades," said O'Gillicuddy.

"But shades are not abroad in daylight."

"That is a human fallacy," said O'Gillicuddy. "We cannot, of course, be seen in daylight. But neither can we be at night if it is not our wish."

The other shades made mutters of agreement.

"We'll make up our packs," said Cynthia, "and leave all the rest behind. Elmer and Bronco will come looking for us here. We'll leave a note for them. We'll pin it to one of the packs, where they'll be sure to see it."

"We'll have to tell them where we're heading," I said. "Does anyone have any idea where we'll be going?"

"Into the mountains," said the census-taker.

"Do you know a river," Cynthia asked, "that is called the Ohio?"

"I know it very well," said the census-taker. "Do you want to go to the Ohio?"

"Now, look here," I said, "we can't go chasing . . ."

"Why not?" asked Cynthia. "If we're going somewhere we might as well go where we wish to go . . ."

"But I thought that we agreed . . ."

"I know," said Cynthia. "You made it very plain. Your composition has first claim and I suppose it still will have to have it. But you can make it anywhere, can't you?"

"Certainly. Within reason."

"All right," said Cynthia. "We'll head toward the Ohio. If that is all right with you," she said to the census-taker.

"It's all right with me," he said. "We'll have to cross the

116

mountains to reach the river. I hope we can lose the wolves somewhere in the mountains. But if I may inquire . . ."

"It's a long story," I told him curtly. "We can tell you later."

"Have you ever heard," asked Cynthia, "of an immortal man who lives a hermit's life?"

She never let go of anything once she got her claws in it.

"I think I have," said the census-taker. "Very long ago. I suspect it was a myth. Earth had so many myths."

"But not any longer," I said.

He shook his head, rather sadly. "No longer. All Earth's myths are dead."

14

The sky had clouded over and the wind had shifted to the north, growing cold and sharp. Despite the chill, there was a strange, wet smell in the air. The pine trees that grew along the slope threshed and moaned.

My watch had stopped, not that it made much difference. It had been fairly useless ever since leaving Alden. On board the funeral ship, which operated on galactic time, it had been impossible. And Earth time, it had turned out, was not the same as Alden time, although with a little mathematical calculation one could get along. I had inquired about the time at the settlement where we'd waited for the hoedown, but no one seemed to know or care. So far as I could learn, there was only one clock in the settlement, a rather crude, homemade affair, made mostly out of carved wood, that more than half the time stood dead and silent because no one ever seemed to think to wind it. So I'd set my watch by the sun, but had missed the moment when it stood directly overhead and had been compelled to estimate how long since it had started its decline to the west. Now it had stopped and I could not get it started. Why I bothered I don't know; I was as well off without it.

The census-taker clumped on ahead, with Cynthia behind him and myself bringing up the rear. We had covered a lot of ground since dawn, although how long we had been walking I had no way of knowing. The sun was covered by the clouds and my watch had stopped and there was no way to know the time of day.

There was no sign of the ghosts, although I had the queasy feeling they were not far away. And the census-taker troubled me as much as the invisible ghosts, for in the daylight he was a most disturbing thing. Seen face to face, he was not human unless one could regard a rag doll as being human. For his face was a rag-doll face, with a pinched mouth that was slightly askew, eyes that gave the impression of a cross-stitch and no nose or chin at all. His face ran straight down into his neck with no intervening jaw, and the cowl and robe that I had taken for clothing, when one had a close look at him, seemed a part of his grotesque body. If it had not seemed so improbable, one would have been convinced that they were his body. Whether he had feet I didn't know, for the robe (or body) came down so close to the ground that his feet were covered. He moved as if he had feet, but there was no sign of them and I found myself wondering, if he had no feet, how he managed to move along so well. Move he did. He set a brisk pace, bobbling along ahead of us. It was all that we could do to keep up with him.

He had not spoken since we had started, but had simply led the way, with the two of us following and neither of us speaking, either, for at the pace that we were going we didn't have the breath to speak.

The way was wild, an unbroken wilderness with no sign that it ever had been occupied by man, as it surely must have been at one time. We followed the ridgetops for miles, at times descending from them to cross a small valley, then climb a series of hills again to follow other ridgetops. From the ridges we could see vast stretches of the countryside, but nowhere was there a clearing. We found no ruins, saw no crumbling chimneys, ran across no ancient fence rows. Down in the valleys the woods stood thick and heavy; on the ridgetops the trees thinned out to some extent. It was a rocky land; huge boulders lay strewn all about and great gray outcroppings of rock jutted from the hillsides. There was a little life. A few birds flew chirping among the trees

119

and occasionally there were small life forms I recognized as rabbits and squirrels, but they were not plentiful.

We had stopped briefly to drink from shallow streams that ran through the valleys we had crossed, but the stops had been only momentary, long enough to lie flat upon our bellies and gulp a few mouthfuls of water, while the census-taker (who did not seem to need to drink) waited impatiently, and then we hurried on.

Now, for the first time since we had set out, we halted. The ridge we had been traveling rose to a high point and then sloped down for a distance and on this high point lay a scattered jumble of barn-size rocks, grouped together in a rather haphazard fashion, as if some ancient giant had held a fistful of them and had been playing with them, as a boy will play with marbles, but having gotten tired of them, had dropped them here, where they had remained. Stunted pine trees grew among them, clutching for desperate footholds with twisted, groping roots.

The census-taker, who was a few yards ahead of us, scrambled up a path when he reached the jumble of rocks, disappearing into them. We followed where he'd gone and found him crouched in a pocket formed by massive stones. It was a place protected from the bitter wind, but open in the direction we had come so that we could see back along our trail.

He motioned for us to join him.

"We shall rest for a little time," he said. "Perhaps you'd like to eat. But no fire. Perhaps a fire tonight. We'll see."

I didn't want to eat. I simply wanted to sit down and never move again.

"Maybe we should keep on," said Cynthia. "They may be after us."

She didn't look as if she wanted to keep on. She looked wore down to a nubbin.

The prissy little mouth in the rag-doll face said, "They have not returned to the cave as yet."

"How do you know?" I asked.

"The shades," he said. "They would let me know. I haven't heard from them."

"Maybe they've run out on us," I said.

He shook his head. "They would not do that," he said. "Where is there to run to?"

"I don't know," I said. I couldn't, for the life of me, imagine where a ghost might run to.

Cynthia sat down wearily and leaned back against the side of a massive boulder that towered far above her. "In that case," she said, "we can afford a rest."

She had slid her pack off her shoulder before sitting down. Now she pulled it over to her, unstrapped it and rummaged around inside of it. She took something out of it and handed it to me. There were three or four strips of hard and brittle stuff, red shading into black.

"What is this junk?" I asked.

"That junk," she said, "is jerky. Dessicated meat. You break off a chunk of it and put it in your mouth and chew it. It is very nourishing."

She offered a few sticks to the census-taker, but he pushed it away. "I ingest food very sparingly," he said.

I unshipped my pack and sat down beside her. I broke off a chunk of jerky and put it in my mouth. It felt like a piece of cardboard, only harder and perhaps not quite as tasty.

I sat there and chewed very gingerly and stared back along the way we'd come and thought what a far cry Earth was from our gentle world of Alden. I don't think that in that moment I quite regretted leaving Alden, but I was not too far from it. I recalled that I had read of Earth and dreamed of it and yearned for it, and so help me, here it was. I admitted to myself that I was no woodsman and that while I could appreciate a piece of woodland beauty as well as any man, I was not equipped, either physically or temperamentally, to take on the sort of primitive world Earth had turned out to be. This was not the sort of thing I'd bargained for and I didn't like it, but under the circumstances there wasn't much I could do about it.

Cynthia was busy chewing, too, but now she stopped to ask a question. "Are we heading toward the Ohio?"

"Oh, yes, indeed," said the census-taker, "but we're still some distance from it."

"And the immortal hermit?"

"I know naught," said the census-taker, "of an immortal hermit. Except some stories of him. And there are many stories."

"Monster stories?" I asked.

"I do not understand."

"You said that once there were monsters and implied the wolves were used against them. I have wondered ever since."

"It was long ago."

"But they once were here."

"Yes, once."

"Genetic monsters?"

"This word you use . . ."

"Look," I said, "ten thousand years ago this planet was a radioactive hell. Many life forms died. Many of those that lived had genetic damage."

"I do not know," he said.

The hell you don't, I told myself. And the suspicion swiftly crossed my mind that the reason he did not want to know was that he, himself, was one of those genetic monsters and was well aware of it. I wondered dully why I had not thought of it before.

I kept at him. "Why should Cemetery care about the monsters? Why was it necessary to fabricate the wolves to hunt them down? I suppose that is what the wolves were used for."

"Yes," he said. "Thousands of them. Great packs of them. They were programmed to hunt down monsters."

"Not humans," I said. "Only monsters."

"That is right. Only the monsters."

"I suppose there might have been times they made mistakes, when they hunted humans as well as monsters. It

122

would be hard to program robots that only hunted monsters."

"There were mistakes," the census-taker said.

"And I don't suppose," said Cynthia, bitterly, "that Cemetery cared too much. When something of the sort did occur, they didn't really mind."

"I would not know," said the census-taker.

"What I don't understand," said Cynthia, "is why they should have done it. What difference did a few monsters make?"

"There were not a few of them."

"Well, then, a lot of them."

"I think," said the census-taker, "that it might have been the Pilgrim business. Once Cemetery had gotten off to a solid start, the Pilgrim business grew until it represented a fair piece of revenue. And you could not have a pack of howling monsters come tearing down the land when Pilgrims were around. It would have scared them off. The word would have spread and there would have been fewer Pilgrims."

"Oh, lovely," Cynthia said. "A program of genocide. I suppose the monsters have been fairly well wiped out."

"Yes," said the census-taker, "fairly well disposed of."

"With a few showing up," I said, "only now and then."

His cross-stitch eyes crinkled at me and I wished I hadn't said it. I don't know what was wrong with me. Here we were, depending on this little jerk to help us, and I was needling him.

I cut out the talking and went back to chewing jerky. It had softened up a bit and had a salty-smoky taste and even if it wasn't supplying too much nourishment, it still gave me the impression that I was eating something.

We sat there chewing, the two of us, while the census-taker just sat, not doing anything.

I looked around at Cynthia. "How are you getting on?" I asked.

"I'll do all right," she said, a little sharply.

123

"I'm sorry it turned out this way," I said. "It is not what I had in mind."

"Of course it's not," she said. "You thought of it as a polite little jaunt to a romantic planet, made romantic by what you'd read of it and imagined of it and . . ."

"I came here to make a composition," I said, considerably nettled at her, "not to play hide-and-seek with bomb-throwers and grave-robbers and a pack of robot wolves."

"And you're blaming me for it. If I hadn't been along, if I hadn't foisted myself off on you . . ."

"Hell, no," I said. "I never thought of that."

"But even if you did," she said, "it would be all right, for you'd be doing it for good old Thorney . . ."

"Cut it out," I shouted at her, really burned up now. "What's got into you? What's this all about?"

Before she could answer the census-taker got to his feet (that is, if he had feet); at any rate, he rose.

"It is time to go again," he said. "You've had rest and nourishment and now we must push on."

The wind had become sharper and colder. As we moved out of the shelter of the nest of boulders and faced the barren ridgetop, it struck us like a knife and the first few drops of driven rain spattered in our faces.

We pushed ahead—pushing against the rain, leaning into it. It was as if a great hand had been placed against us and tried to hold us back. It didn't seem to bother the census-taker much; he skipped on ahead without any trouble. The funny thing about it was that the wind seemed to have no effect at all upon his robe; it didn't flutter, it never even stirred, it stayed just the way it was, hanging to the ground.

I would have liked to call this to Cynthia's attention, but when I tried to yell at her, the buffeting wind blew the words back into my mouth.

From below us came the moaning of the forest trees, bending in the gale. Birds tried to fly and were whipped

124

about the sky. The cloud cover seemed to become thicker by the minute, although as far as I could see, there were no moving clouds. The rain came in sudden gusts, icy cold, hard against the face.

We trudged on, miserably. I lost all track of everything. I kept my eyes on Cynthia's plodding figure as she moved on ahead of me. Once she stumbled and without a word I helped her up. Without a word, she resumed the march.

Now the rain came down without a letup, driven by the wind. At intervals it turned to ice and rattled in the branches of the trees. Then it would turn to rain again and the rain, it seemed to me, was colder than the ice.

We walked forever and then I found that we were no longer on a ridge, but were slanting down a slope. We reached a creek and found a narrow place where we could jump across it and started clambering up the opposite slope. Suddenly the ground leveled off beneath my feet and I heard the census-taker saying, "This is far enough."

As soon as I heard those words I let my legs buckle under me and sat down on solid rock. For a moment I paid no attention to where we were. It was quite enough that there was no longer any need to move. But gradually I became aware of what was going on.

We had stopped, I saw, on a broad, flat shelf of rock that extended out in front of a huge rock shelter. The roof of the shelter, some thirty feet or more above the shelf, flared back to form a deep niche in the face of a jutting cliff. The slab of rock extending out from the cliff ran back into the shelter, forming a level floor of stone. A few feet downward from the shelf, the creek flowed down the valley, forming little pools and rapids, pinching down, then broadening out, a little mountain stream that was in a hurry, foaming in the rapids and then resting in the pools before it took another plunge. Beyond the stream the hill rose steeply to the ridgetop along which we'd come.

"Here we are," said the census-taker in a happy, chirpy voice. "Snug against the night and weather. We will build a fire and catch some trout out of the stream and wish the wolf ill luck in his trailing."

"The wolf?" said Cynthia. "There were three wolves to start with. What happened to the other two?"

"I have intelligence," said the census-taker, "that but one remains. It seems the others met with awkward accidents."

15

Beyond the shelter's mouth the storm raged in the night. The fire gave light and warmth and our clothes at last were dry and there had been, as the census-taker had said, fish to be gotten in the brook, beautiful speckled trout that had made a welcome break from the gook we had been eating out of cans and a vast improvement over jerky.

We were not the first to use the shelter. Our fire had been built on a blackened circle on the stone, where the fires of earlier years (although how long ago there was no way of knowing) had chipped and flaked the surface of the rock. Along the broad expanse of stone were several other similarly blackened areas, half camouflaged by a scattering of blown autumn leaves.

In a pile of leaves, wedged and caught far back in the rocky cleft, where the roof plunged down to meet the floor, Cynthia had found another evidence of human occupancy—a metal rod some four feet long, an inch in diameter, and touched only here and there with rust.

I sat beside the fire, staring at the flames, thinking back along the trail and trying to figure out how such well-laid plans as ours could have gone so utterly astray. The answer was, of course, that Cemetery had been responsible, although perhaps not responsible for our meeting with the band of grave robbers. We had simply stumbled onto them.

I tried to figure exactly where we stood and it seemed, as I thought about it, we did not stand well at all. We had been harried from the settlement and we had been split up and Cynthia and I had fallen into the hands of an enigmatic being that might be little better than a mad-man.

Now there was the wolf—one wolf if what the census-taker said was right. There was no doubt in my mind what had happened to the other two. They had caught up with Elmer and the Bronco and that had been a great mistake for them. But while Elmer had been dismantling two of them, the third one had escaped and probably even now was upon our trail—if there were a trail to follow. We had gone along high, barren ridges, with a strong wind blowing to wipe away our scent. Now, with the breaking of the storm, there might be no trail at all to follow.

"Fletch," said Cynthia, "what are you thinking of?"

"I am wondering," I said, "where Elmer and Bronco might be at this moment."

"They're on their way back to the cave," she said. "They will find the note."

"Sure," I said, "the note. A lot of good the note will do. We are traveling northwest, it said. If you don't catch up with us before we reach there, you'll find us on the Ohio River. Do you realize how much land may lie northwest before you reach the river and how big that river is?"

"It was the best that we could do," she said, rather angrily.

"We shall, in the morning," said the census-taker, "build a fire, high upon a ridge, to make a signal. We will guide them to us."

"Them," I said, "and everyone else in sight, perhaps even including the wolf. Or is it still three wolves?"

"It is only one," said the census-taker, "and one wolf would not be so brave. Wolves are brave only when in packs."

"I don't think," I said, "I would care to meet even one, lone, cowardly wolf."

"There are few of them now," said the census-taker. "They have not been loosed to hunt for years. The long years of confinement may have taken a lot of the sharpness from them."

128

"What I want to know," I said, "is how it took Cemetery so long to send them out against us. They could have turned them loose the minute that we left."

"Undoubtedly," said the census-taker, "they had to send for them. I don't know where they are kept, but doubtless at some distance."

The wind went whooping down the valley that lay in front of us and a sheet of rain came hissing into the mouth of the cave to spatter on the rock just beyond the fire.

"Where are all your pals?" I asked. "Where are all the shades?"

"On a night like this," said the census-taker, "they have far-ranging business."

I didn't ask what kind of business. I didn't want to know.

"I don't know about the rest of you," said Cynthia, "but I'm going to roll up in my blanket and try to get some sleep."

"Both of you might as well," said the census-taker. "It has been a long, hard day. I will keep the watch. I almost never sleep."

"You never sleep," I said, "and you almost never eat. The wind doesn't blow that robe of yours. Just what the hell are you?"

He didn't answer. I knew he wouldn't answer.

The last thing that I saw before I went to sleep was the census-taker sitting a short distance from the fire, a rigid upright figure that had a strange resemblance to a cone resting on its base.

I woke cold. The fire had gone out and beyond the cave mouth dawn was breaking. The storm had stopped and what I could see of the sky was clear.

And there, on the rock shelf that extended out in front of the cave, sat a metal wolf. He was hunkered on his haunches and he was looking straight at me and from his steel jaws dangled the limp form of a rabbit.

I sat up rapidly, the blanket falling from me, putting out my hand to find a stick of firewood, although what good a stick of wood would have done against a monster such as that I had no idea. But in grasping for the stick, I found something else. I wasn't looking where I was reaching out because I didn't dare take my eyes off the wolf. But when my fingers touched it, I knew what I had—the four-foot metal rod that Cynthia had unearthed from beneath the pile of leaves. I wrapped my fingers around it with something like a prayer of thankfulness and got carefully to my feet, holding the rod so tight that the grip was painful.

The wolf made no move toward me; it just stayed sitting there, with that silly rabbit hanging from its jaws. I had forgotten that it had a tail, but now its tail began to beat, very gently, very slowly upon the slab of rock, for all the world like the tail-beating of a dog that was glad to see someone.

I looked around quickly. The census-taker was nowhere to be seen, but Cynthia was sitting upright in her blanket and her eyes were the size of saucers. She didn't notice that I was looking at her; she had her eyes fastened on the wolf.

I took a step sidewise to get around the fire and as I did I lifted the metal rod to a ready position. If I could get in just one lucky lick, I thought, upon that ugly head when it came at me, I stood at least some chance.

But the wolf didn't come at me. It just sat there and when I took another step it keeled over on its back and stayed there, with all four feet sticking in the air, and now its tail beat a wild tattoo upon the stone, the sound of the metal beating on the stone ringing in the morning silence.

"It wants to be friendly," Cynthia said. "It is asking you not to hit it."

I took another step.

"And look," said that silly Cynthia, "it has brought a rabbit for us."

I lowered the rod and kept it low and now the wolf turned over on its belly and began creeping toward me. I stood and waited for it. When it got close enough, it dropped the rabbit at my feet.

"Pick it up," said Cynthia.

"Pick it up," I said, "and it will take off my arm."

130

"Pick it up," she said. "It has brought the rabbit to you. It has given it to you."

So I stooped and picked up that crazy rabbit and the moment that I did, the wolf leaped up with a wriggling joy and rubbed against my legs so hard it almost tipped me over.

16

We sat beside the fire and gnawed the last shreds of meat off the rabbit's bones, while the wolf lay off to one side, its tail beating occasionally on the stony floor, watching us intently.

"What do you suppose happened to him?" Cynthia asked.

"He maybe went insane," I said. "Or turned chicken after what happened to the other two. Or he may just be laying for us, lulling us to sleep. When he has the chance he'll finish off the two of us."

I reached out and pulled the metal rod just a little closer.

"I don't think that at all," said Cynthia. "You know what I think. He doesn't want to go back."

"Back to where?"

"Back to wherever it is that Cemetery keeps him. Think of it. He and the other wolves, however many there may be, may have been kept penned up for years and . . ."

"They wouldn't keep them penned," I said. "More likely they would turn them off until they needed them."

"Then maybe that is it," she said. "Maybe he doesn't want to go back because he knows they'll turn him off."

I grunted at her. It was all damn foolishness. Maybe the best thing to do, I thought, was to pick up the metal rod and beat the wolf to death. The only thing, I guess, that stopped me was a suspicion that the wolf might take a lot of killing and that in the process I'd come out second best.

"I wonder what happened to the census-taker," I said.

"The wolf scared him off," said Cynthia. "He won't be coming back."

"He could at least have wakened us. Given us a chance."

"It turned out all right."

"But he couldn't know it would."

"What do we do now?"

"I don't know," I said. And that was exactly right. I really didn't know. Never in my life had I felt so unsure of what my next step should be. I had no real idea of where we were; we were lost, as far as I was concerned, in a howling wilderness. We were separated from the two stronger members of our party and our guide had deserted us. A metal wolf had made friends with us and I was far from sure of the sincerity of its friendship.

I caught the motion out of the corner of my eye and leaped to my feet, but there was nothing I could do about it except stand there and stare into the muzzles of the guns. Holding the guns were two men and one of them I recognized as the big brute who had stood in the forefront of the mob that Cynthia and I had faced, futile clubs in hand, back at the campsite of the ghouls just before Elmer had come bursting in to break up the confrontation. I was a bit surprised that I recognized him, for at the time I had been too busy watching all the others that made up the mob who had left off their attack on Bronco to zero in on us. But now I found that I did know him—the leering half-smile pasted on his face, the droopy eye, that ragged scar that ran across one cheek. The other one I did not recognize.

They had crept up to one corner of the cave and now they stood there, with their rifles pointed at us.

I heard Cynthia gasp in surprise and I said sharply to her, "Stay down. Don't move."

With a scratch of metal claws on rock, something came up to me and stood beside me, pressing hard against my leg. I didn't look to see what it might be. I knew. It was Wolf, lining up with me against the guns.

The two with the guns apparently had not seen him, lying off to one side of us. And now that he moved into their view, the leering smile came off Big Brute's face and

133

his jaw sagged just a little. A nervous tic ran across the face of the other man. But they stood their ground.

"Gentlemen," I said, "it appears to me a stand-off. You could kill us easy, but you wouldn't live to get a hundred feet."

They kept their guns pointed at us, but finally Big Brute lifted his and let the butt slide to the ground.

"Jed," he said, "put up your shooting iron. These folks have outsmarted us."

Jed lowered his gun.

"It seems to me," said Big Brute, "that we have to cipher out a way for all of us to get out of this scrape without losing any hide."

"Come on in," I said, "but be careful of the guns."

They came up to the fire, walking slowly and somewhat sheepishly.

I took a quick glance at Cynthia. She still was crouched upon the floor, but she wasn't scared. She was hard as nails.

"Fletch," she said, "the gentlemen must be hungry, coming all this way. Why don't you ask them to sit down while I open up a can or two. We haven't too much, traveling light, but I put in some stew."

The two of them looked at me and I nodded rather curtly.

"Please do," I said.

They sat down and laid their guns beside them.

Wolf didn't stir; he stood and looked at them.

Big Brute made a questioning gesture at him.

"He's all right," I said. "Just don't make any sudden moves."

I hoped that I was right. I couldn't quite be sure.

Cynthia, digging into one of the packs, had a stew pan out. I poked the fire together and it blazed up brightly.

"Now," I said, "suppose you tell me what this is all about?"

"You stole our horses," Big Brute said.

Jed said, "We were hunting them."

I shook my head. "You could have followed the trail

134

blindfolded. You should have had no trouble. There were a lot of horses."

"Well," said Big Brute, "we found the place where you hid out and we found the note. Jed here, he was able to get it puzzled out. And we knew about this cave."

"It's a camping place," said Jed. "We camp here ourselves, every now and then."

It still didn't make too much sense, but I didn't press it. Big Brute, however, went on to explain. "We figured you weren't alone. Someone must have been with you. Someone who knew the country. People like you wouldn't strike out on your own. And this place here is a hard day's march."

Jed said, "What I can't figure is the wolf. We never counted on no wolf. We thought by this time he'd be halfway home."

"You knew about the wolves?"

"We saw the tracks. Three of them. And we found what was left of the other two."

"Not you," I said. "You came straight from the place where we slept. You had to. You wouldn't have had the time . . ."

"Not us," said Jed. "We didn't see it. Some of the rest of us. They let us know."

"They let you know?"

"Sure," said Big Brute. "We keep one another posted."

"Telepathy," said Cynthia, softly. "It has to be telepathy."

"But telepathy . . ."

"A survival factor," she said. "The people who were left on Earth after the war would have needed survival factors. And with mutations, there might have been a lot of factors. Fine things to have if they didn't kill you first. Telepathy would have been good to have and it would not have killed you."

"Tell me," I said to Big Brute, "what happened to Elmer—to the other two who were with us?"

"The metal things," said Jed.

135

"That's right. The metal things."

Big Brute shook his head.

"You mean that you don't know?"

"We can find out."

"Well, then, you find out."

"Look, mister," said Jed, "we need a bargaining point. This is our bargaining point."

"The wolf is ours," I said. "And the wolf's right here."

"Maybe we shouldn't be sitting here dickering," said Big Brute. "Maybe we should throw in together."

"That's why you came sneaking up on us, to throw in with us?"

"Well, no," said Jed. "Not exactly. We had blood in our eye, for sure. You busted up our camp and run us off and then you took our horses. There ain't nothing more low-down than running off a man's horses. We weren't feeling very friendly, to tell the truth."

"But things have changed now. You are willing to be friendly?"

"Look at it this way," said Big Brute. "Someone set the wolves on you and the only ones who could have sent out the wolves was Cemetery and we sort of calculate anyone Cemetery doesn't like has to be a friend of ours."

"What have you got against Cemetery?" Cynthia asked. She had moved over to the fire, standing beside Big Brute, with the stew pan in her hand. "You've been stealing from Cemetery. You've been digging up the graves. Seems to me you would be out of business if it wasn't for Cemetery."

"They don't play fair," Jed whined. "They set traps for us. All sorts of wicked traps. They cause us all sorts of trouble."

Big Brute was still bewildered. "How come you made up with that wolf?" he asked. "Those things aren't supposed to make friends with anyone. They're man-killers, every one of them."

Cynthia was still standing beside Big Brute, but she wasn't looking at him. She was looking across the creek to

136

the hill. I wondered rather idly what she was looking at, but it was only a passing thought.

"If you want to throw in with us," I said, "how about beginning by telling us where to find the metal beings."

I didn't really trust them; I knew we couldn't trust them. But I thought it was worth going along with them a ways if they could give us some idea of Elmer and Bronco's whereabouts.

"I don't know," said Big Brute. "I honestly don't know if we should tell you that or not."

Out of the corner of my eye, I saw Cynthia move. Her arm came up and I saw what she meant to do, although I couldn't understand, for the life of me, why she was doing it. There was no way for me to stop her, and even if there were, I would not have done it, for I knew she must have good reason. There was only one thing for me to do and I did it. I lunged for Jed's rifle, which lay on the rocky floor beside him and as I moved, Cynthia brought the stew pan down as hard as she could manage, on top of Big Brute's head.

Jed snatched at his gun, both of us grabbing hold of it. We rose to our feet, both of us hanging onto it, wrestling for it, trying to jerk it from the other's grasp.

Events were happening much too fast for me to take any lasting notice of them. I saw Cynthia, Big Brute's rifle clutched in her hands and at the ready. Big Brute was crawling around the floor on his hands and knees, shaking his head, as if he were attempting to rattle his brains back together into a solid mass, and a little way beyond him the stew pan lay canted on its side, battered out of shape. Wolf was a streak of churning silver, racing across the cave, heading for the entrance, and out on the opposite hillside dark figures were running. And somewhere out there, too, dull pops were sounding and humming bees came into the cave to thud against its walls.

Jed's face was all twisted up, either in fear or anger (I could not decide which, but, strangely, in the midst of all

137

that was going on, I found the time to wonder). His mouth was open, as if he might be yelling, but he wasn't yelling. His teeth were yellowed fangs and his breath was foul. He wasn't as big as I was, nor as heavy, but he was a wiry customer, quick and tough and full of fight, and I knew, even as I fought for it, that he'd finally get that gun away from me.

Big Brute had tottered to his feet and was backing slowly away from the fire, staring with horrified fascination at Cynthia, who pointed his rifle at him.

It all seemed to have gone on for a long while, although I don't imagine it had been more than a few seconds, and it seemed as if it might keep on forever. Then, quite suddenly, Jed buckled in the middle. He loosed his grip on the gun and slid sidewise, tumbling to the floor, and I saw then the slow seep of red that stained his back.

Cynthia yelled at me, "Fletch, let's get away! They are shooting at us!"

But they were, I saw, not shooting any longer. They were fleeing for their lives, small dark figures of leaping, dodging men scrambling up the hillside. Two or three of them, I saw, were busily climbing trees. Up the hill, after them, flashed a steel machine and as I watched, it caught one of them in its sharp, steel jaws and shook the body for an instant before it tossed it to one side.

There was no sign of Big Brute. He had gotten clean away.

"Fletch, we can't stay here," said Cynthia, and I quite agreed with her. It was no place to stay, with the ghouls snapping at our heels. Now, while Wolf had them on the run, was the time to get away.

She already had reached one corner of the cave and was scrambling down the hillside, and I followed her. I lost my footing on the steepness of the rubble and, flat upon my back, skidded almost to the creek before I could gain my feet again. When I fell I dropped the gun and was turning back to get it when something went buzzing past my ear and threw up a small spurt of earth and rock on the inclined bank not more than three feet ahead of me. I rolled over rapidly and looked up to the ridge. A puff of blue smoke was floating up from a tree where a scarecrow figure crouched.

I forgot about the gun.

Cynthia was running down the narrow hollow that carried the creek and I ran after her. Behind me a couple of guns went off, but the balls must have flown far wide of us, for I didn't hear them hum nor did I see them strike. In a few more seconds, I told myself, we'd be out of range. Homemade guns carrying balls of lead powered by homemade powder could not have had much carrying power.

The narrow valley was tortuous traveling. The hills came down steeply on either side, in a sharp V formation, and there was no level ground. The surface was cluttered by massive boulders that through the ages had come rolling down the hillsides. In some places gigantic trees grew in the narrowness of the notch between the hills. There was no sort of trail to follow; nothing in its right mind would travel down this valley short of sheer necessity. It was a matter of finding the best path that one could, dodging around the rocks and trees, leaping the brook when it swung across one's path.

I caught up with Cynthia when she was slowed down by an enormous pile of boulders, and after that we went together. I saw that she didn't have Big Brute's gun.

"I dropped it," she said. "It was heavy. It kept getting in my way."

"It's just as well," I said. And it was just as well. Each of the guns carried a single charge and we had no balls or powder to reload (even if we'd known how to reload) once that charge was fired. They were awkward things to handle and I had a hunch a man would have to do a lot of shooting with them before he could come anywhere near hitting what he was aiming at.

139

We came to a place where another little V-shaped valley came into the one we had been following.

"Let's go up that one," Cynthia said. "They know we came down this one."

I nodded. If they followed, they might suspect we had chosen the easier course, continuing down the hollow from the cave.

"Fletch," she said, "we haven't got a thing. We ran off without our packs."

I hesitated. "I could go back," I said. "You go on up the hollow. I'll catch up with you."

"We can't separate again," she said. "We have to stick together. None of this would have happened if we'd stayed with Elmer."

"Wolf has got them treed," I said. "Either treed or running."

"No," she said. "Some of them up the trees have guns. And there are too many of them for Wolf to handle. They'll scatter. He can't chase them all."

"You saw them," I said. "That's why you hit the big one with the pan."

"I saw them," she said, "slithering down the hillside. But I might have hit him anyhow. We couldn't trust them, Fletch. And you aren't going back. I'd have to go with you and I am scared to go."

I gave in. I couldn't honestly decide whether it was giving in or not wanting to go back, myself.

"Later on," I said. "Later on, when this is all over, we can come back and get the stuff." Knowing that we probably never would. Or that it might not be there if we did go back.

We started up the hollow. It was as bad as the one we had come down; worse because now we were climbing.

I let Cynthia go ahead and I did some worrying. We must have been in a real panic, both of us, when we left the cave. It would have been simple, using no more than a minute's time, to have grabbed up the packs. But we hadn't

140

done it and now we were without food and blankets, without anything at all. Except fire, I thought. I had the lighter in my pocket. I felt a little better, although not much, when I realized we still had fire.

The way was grueling and there were times when we had to stop to rest. Listening for some sound back at the cave, I heard nothing and began to wonder, rather dazedly, if what I remembered had really happened there. I knew, of course, it had.

We were nearing the top of the ridge and the valley petered out. We clambered to the crest. The ridge was heavily wooded and when we reached the top, we were in a fairyland of beauty. The trees were massive blocks of red and yellow and in some of them were climbing vines that provided slashes of deep gold and brilliant crimson. The day was clear and warm. Looking at the color, I remembered that first day—only a few days ago, but seeming more like weeks—when we had left the Cemetery and gone down the hill to the first autumn-painted forest I had ever seen.

We stood, watching back the way that we had come.

"Why should they be hunting us?" asked Cynthia. "Sure, we took their horses, but if that is all it is, they should be hunting the horses and not us."

"Revenge, maybe," I said. "A twisted idea of getting even with us. Probably only a part of them are after us. The others must be following the horses."

"That may be it," she said, "but I can't bring myself to think so. There is something more than that."

"It's Cemetery," I said and I wasn't entirely clear what I meant by saying it, although it did seem that Cemetery was somehow involved in everything that happened. But as soon as I said it, the whole pattern formed inside my mind.

"Don't you see," I said. "Cemetery has a finger in everything that happens. They can bring certain pressures. Back at the settlement someone got a case of whiskey for trying to blow up Bronco. And here are the ghouls . . ."

"But the ghouls," she said, "are different. They're stealing from Cemetery. Cemetery is setting traps for them. They'd make no deals with Cemetery."

"Look," I said, "it may be they're only trying to curry some favor with Cemetery. They found the wolves were after us and who but Cemetery would set the wolves on us. And the wolves had failed. To the kinds of minds the ghouls have it must have seemed a rather simple thing, an opportunity. If, the wolves having failed, they could bring in our heads there might be something in it for them. It's as simple as all that."

"It could be," she said. "Heaven knows, it gets down to simple basics."

"In which case," I said, "we'd best be getting on."

We went down the slope and struck another rock-littered ravine and followed it until it joined another valley, this one a little wider and easier for traveling.

We found a tree that was almost buried beneath a great grapevine and I clambered up it. Birds and little animals had been at the grapes, but I found a few bunches that carried most of their fruit. Picking them, I dropped them through the branches to the ground. The grapes proved somewhat sour, but we didn't mind too much. We were hungry and they helped to fill us up, but I knew that we'd somehow have to manage something other than grapes. We had no fishhooks, but I did have a jacknife and we probably could cut willow branches and rig up a brush seine that would net some fish for us. We had no salt, I remembered, but hungry enough, we could manage without salt.

"Fletch," said Cynthia, "do you think we ever will find Elmer?"

"Maybe Elmer will find us," I aid. "He must be looking for us."

"We left the note," she said.

"The note is gone," I reminded her. "The ghouls found the note, remember? They'd not have left it for him."

The valley was a little wider than the one we had followed from the cave, but it never broadened out.

142

Rather, the hills seemed to get larger and move in on us. Now there were great rock cliffs that rose a hundred feet or more on either side. It became a less pleasant valley. Progressively, it grew more eerie and frightening. Not only was it stark, but silent. The creek that flowed through it was broad and deep, and there were no shallows or rapids. The water did not talk; it surged along with a look of terrible power.

The sun was low in the west and with some surprise I realized that we had traveled through the day. I was tired, but not tired enough, it seemed, to have walked all day long.

Ahead of us I saw a cleft cutting back into a cliff. The crest of the cliff was crowned with massive trees and occasional ragged cedars clung precariously to its face.

"Let's take a look," I said. "We'll have to find a place to spend the night."

"We'll be cold," she said. "We left the blankets."

"We have fire," I said.

She shuddered. "Can we have a fire? Is it safe to have a fire?"

"We have to have a fire," I told her.

The cleft was dark. The walls of stone enclosed it and we could not see to the end of it because the dark deepened as the fissure ran back into the rock. The floor was pebbles, but off to one side, a little back from the entrance, a slab of rock was raised somewhat above the floor.

"I'll get wood," I said.

"Fletch!"

"We have to have a fire," I said. "We have to chance it. We'll freeze to death without it."

"I'm scared," she said.

I looked at her. In the darkness her face was a blur of whiteness.

"Finally I am scared," she said. "I thought I wouldn't be. I told myself I wouldn't be. I said to me I'd tough it out. And it was all right as long as we were moving and out in the bright sunlight. But now night is coming, Fletch, and we haven't any food and we don't know where we are . . ."

I moved close to her and took her in my arms and she came into them willingly enough. Her arms went around me and clutched me tightly. And for the first time since it all had happened, since that moment I had found her sitting in the car as I walked down the steps from the administration building, I thought of her as a woman and I wondered, with some surprise, why it should have been that way. First, of course, she had been nothing but a nuisance, popping up from nowhere with that ridiculous letter from Thorney clutched tightly in her hand, and since then we'd been run ragged by the events that had come tumbling over one another and there'd been no time in which to think of her as a woman. Rather, she had been a good companion, not doing any bawling, not throwing any fits. I thought somewhat unkindly of myself for the way that I had acted. It would not have hurt me to pay her a few small courtesies along the way, and thinking back, it seemed that I had paid her none.

"We're babes in the woods," she said. "You remember the old Earth fairy tale, of course."

"Sure, I remember it," I said. "The birds came with leaves . . ."

And let it go at that. For the tale, when you came to think of it, was not as pretty as it sounded. I couldn't quite remember, but the birds, it seemed to me, had covered them with leaves because they were quite dead. Like so many other fairy tales, I thought, it was a horror story.

She lifted her head. "I'm all right now," she said. "I'm sorry."

I put my fist underneath her chin and tilted up her face. I bent and kissed her on the lips.

"Now let us go and get the wood," she said.

The sun was nearly gone, but it still was daylight. Lying along the foot of the cliff, we found scattered wood. A lot of it was cedar, dead branches that had fallen off the trees clinging to the bare face of the rock.

"It's a good place to have a fire," I told her. "No one can

see it. They'd have to be directly opposite the opening to see it."

"What about the smoke?" she asked.

"This is dry wood," I said. "There shouldn't be much smoke."

I was right. The wood burned with a bright, clean flame. There was scarcely any smoke. The night chill had not settled in as yet, but we huddled close beside the blaze. It was a friend and comfort. It beat back the dark. It drew us together. It warmed us and made a magic circle for us.

The sun went down and out beyond the cleft dusk closed in rapidly. The world went dark and we were alone.

Something stirred out beyond the circle of the fire, at the outer edge of dark. Something clicked upon the rock.

I leaped erect and then I saw the blur of whiteness. His metal body shining in the firelight, Wolf trotted in to us.

From his steel jaws hung the limp form of a rabbit.

Wolf was hell on rabbits.

17

O'Gillicuddy and his gang arrived when we were finishing off the rabbit. Without salt, it was somewhat short of tasty, but it was food and the only thing we'd had all day had been grapes. Just the fact of eating made life seem a bit more stable and ourselves not entirely lost.

Wolf lay between us, close beside the fire, stretched out, with his massive head resting on his metal paws.

"If he'd only talk," said Cynthia, "it would be very nice. Probably he could tell us what was going on."

"Wolves don't talk," I said, chewing the shinbone of the rabbit.

"But robots do," she said. "Elmer talks. Even Bronco talks. And Wolf here really is a robot. He isn't any wolf. He's just made to look like one."

Wolf shifted his eyes around, to look first at one and then the other of us. He didn't say a word, but he beat his metal tail upon the rock and it made a terrible racket.

"Wolves don't beat their tails," she said.

"How do you know that?"

"I read it somewhere. Wolves don't beat or wag their tails. Dogs do. Wolf is more like a dog than a wolf."

"It bothers me," I said. "Here he was, to start with, thirsting for our blood. Suddenly he turns around in his way of thinking and is a pal of ours. It doesn't make much sense."

"I'm beginning to believe," said Cynthia, "that nothing on the Earth really makes much sense."

146

We sat by the fire, enclosed in the magic circle. The firelight flickered and flickered yet again and there seemed to be a strange sense of motion all around.

"We have visitors," Cynthia said quietly.

"It's O'Gillicuddy," I said. "O'Gillicuddy, are you there?"

"We are here," said O'Gillicuddy. "There are many of us. We come to bear you company in this wilderness."

"And to bear us word, perhaps?"

"Yes, indeed. Word we have to bear."

"We would have you know," said Cynthia, "word or not, we are glad to have you here."

Wolf flicked an ear, as if there were a fly, but there wasn't any fly. Even if there had been, it would not have bothered Wolf.

Ghosts, I thought. The place was full of ghosts, the principal one of which was named O'Gillicuddy. Ghosts were here, I thought, and we were accepting them as if they were people or had been people, and that was madness. Under normal circumstance, a ghost was acceptable, but here, under these conditions, they became not only acceptable, but normal.

And, thinking of it, I became aghast at the abnormality of our condition, how awry it was from the quiet beauty of Alden, how distorted even from the mock majesty of Cemetery. For, in fact, those two places seemed abnormal now. We had become so firmly set in the reality of this mad adventure that the ordinary places we had known now seemed strange and far.

"You are not, I fear," O'Gillicuddy was saying, "safely beyond the clutches of the ghouls. They still trail you with much blood thirstiness."

"You mean," I said, "they want our scalps for Cemetery."

"You have plucked forth the naked truth," said O'Gillicuddy.

"But why?" asked Cynthia. "Surely they are not friends of Cemetery."

"No," said O'Gillicuddy, "they are not, indeed. Upon this planet, Cemetery has no friends. And yet there is no one here who would not do most willingly a favor for them, hoping a favor in return. Thus great power corrupts."

"But there is nothing they would want from Cemetery," Cynthia pointed out.

"Not at the moment, perhaps. But a favor deferred is still a favor and one that can be collected later. One can pile up points."

"You said no one would refuse a favor," I said. "How about yourself?"

"In our case," said O'Gillicuddy, "there is a difference. Cemetery can do nothing for us, but what is perhaps of more importance, it can do nothing to us. We hope no favor and we have no fear."

"And you say we aren't safe?"

"They are hunting for you," said O'Gillicuddy. "They will keep on hunting. You handed them defeat this morning and it lies bitter in their mouths. One the steel wolf killed and another died . . ."

"But they shot him themselves," said Cynthia. "A bullet meant for us. It was no fault of ours."

"They still count it against you. There are two dead and there must be accountability. They do not accept the blame. They lay it all on you."

"They'll have a hard time finding us."

"Hard, perhaps," said O'Gillicuddy, "But find you they will. They are woodsmen of the finest. They range like hunting dogs. They read the wilderness like a book. A turned stone, a disturbed leaf, a bruised blade of grass—it says volumes to them."

"Our only hope," said Cynthia, "is to find Elmer and Bronco. If we were together . . ."

"We can tell you where they are," said O'Gillicuddy, "but it's a long, hard way and you would be turning back into the very arms of the raging ghouls. We tried most desperately to reveal ourselves to your two companions so that we could lead them back to you, but for all that we could do they remained unaware of us. It takes a sharper-tuned sensibility than a robot can possess to discover us."

"It all seems pretty hopeless to me," said Cynthia, sounding considerably discouraged. "You can't guide Elmer and Bronco to us and you say the ghouls are sure to find us."

"And that isn't all," said O'Gillicuddy, seeming ghoulishly happy at what he had to tell us. "The Raveners are on the prowl."

"The Raveners?" I asked. "Are there more than one of them?"

"There are two of them."

"You mean war machines?"

"Is that what you call them?"

"That's what Elmer thinks they are."

"But that can't mean anything to us," protested Cynthia. "Surely the war machines are not tied in with Cemetery."

"But they are," said O'Gillicuddy.

"Why?" I asked. "What has Cemetery got they possible could want?"

"Lubricating oil," said O'Gillicuddy.

I'm afraid I groaned at that. It was such a simple thing and yet so logical. It was something that anyone should have thought of. The machines would have built-in power, more than likely nuclear, although I'd never really known, and they would be self-repairing, but the one thing they would need, perhaps the only thing they would need and would not have, would be lubricants.

This would be something that Cemetery wouldn't miss. Cemetery missed no bets at all. They passed up nothing that would make any other factor on the Earth in some way beholden to them.

"And the census-taker," I said. "I suppose he is some way tied into it as well. And, by the way, where is the census-taker?"

"He disappeared," said O'Gillicuddy. "He flitters here and there. He is not really part of us. He is not always with us. We don't know where he is."

149

"Nor what he is?"

"What he is? Why, he's the census-taker."

"That's not what I mean. Is he a human being? Perhaps a mutated human being. There would have been a lot of human mutation. Some good, mostly bad. Although I imagine that over the years a great part of the bad died out. The ghouls have telepathy and God knows what else and the settlers probably have something, too, although we don't know what it is. Even you, for ghosts are not . . ."

"Shades," said O'Gillicuddy.

"All right, then, shades. Shades are not a normal human condition. Maybe there aren't any shades any place except here on Earth. No one knows what happened during those years after the people fled into space. Earth is a different place today than it was then."

"You got off the track," said Cynthia. "You were asking if the census-taker was a Cemetery creature."

"I am sure that he is not," said O'Gillicuddy. "I don't know what he is. I have always thought he was a sort of human being. He is a lot like humans. Not made the way they are, of course, and there is only one of him and . . ."

"Look," I said, "you didn't come here just to bear us company. You came here for a purpose. You wouldn't have come just to bring us bad news. What is it all about?"

"There are many of us here," said the shade. "We foregathered in some strength of numbers. We sent out a call for a gathering of the clan, for we feel great compassion and a strange comradeship with you. Not in all the history of the Earth has anyone before you tweaked the tail of Cemetery in such a hearty fashion."

"And you like that?"

"We like it very much."

"And you've come to cheer us on."

"Not cheer," said O'Gillicuddy, "although that we would also do and most willingly. But we feel that it is in our capacity to be of the slightest help."

"We're in the market," said Cynthia, "for any help there is."

150

"It becomes a complicated matter to explain," said O'Gillicuddy, "and in lack of adequate information, you must fill in with faith. Being the sort of things we are, we have no real contact with the corporeal universe. But it seems we do have some marginal powers to interact with time and space, which are neither in the corporeal universe nor quite out of it."

"Now, wait a second there," I said. "What you are talking of . . ."

"Believe me," said O'Gillicuddy, "we have wracked our mental powers and can come up with nothing else. It is little that we have to offer, but . . ."

"What you propose to do," said Cynthia, "is to move us in time."

"But by only the tiniest fraction," said O'Gillicuddy. "A minute part of a second. Barely out of the present, but that would be quite enough."

"It's never been done," Cynthia objected. "For hundreds of years it has been studied and investigated and absolutely nothing has ever come of it."

"Have you ever done it?" I demanded.

"No, not actually," said O'Gillicuddy. "But we have thought about it and speculated on it and we are rather sure . . ."

"But not entirely sure?"

"You are right," said O'Gillicuddy. "Not entirely sure."

"And once you've done it," I asked, "how about our getting back? I would not want to live out my life a fractional part of a second behind all the universe."

"We have worked that out, too," the shade said blithely. "We would set a time-trap at the entrance of this cleft and by stepping into it . . ."

"But you're not sure of that one, either."

"Well, fairly certain," said O'Gillicuddy.

It wasn't very promising and, on top of that, I asked myself, how could we be sure that any of the rest of all he'd told was the truth? Maybe O'Gillicuddy and his gang of shades were doing no more than trying to push us into a situation where we'd serve willingly as subjects for an experiment they had cooked up. And, come to think of it, how could we be sure there were any shades at all? We had seen them, or seemed to see them, as they danced around the fire back at the settlement. But actually all we had to go on was what the census-taker had told us and this voice that said it was O'Gillicuddy.

And what about the voice of O'Gillicuddy? Was that imagination, too, as seeing them back at the settlement may have been, or imagining again that we had seen strange shapes back at the cave when they first had come to us? The trouble was that I was not the only one who was hearing it. Cynthia was hearing it as well as I, or she acted as if she did. Either that, or I imagined that she did. It was a hell of a thing, I told myself—to question not only the reality of your environment, but the reality of yourself as well.

"Cynthia," I asked her, "are you really hearing all of this . . ."

The fire exploded in front of us. Ash and fire and burning brands sprayed across the cave and onto us. From outside came a hollow boom and then another and something traveling very fast smacked into the rock behind us.

We leaped to our feet, all three of us, and as we did something boiled inside the space between the rocks. Something—I don't know what it was—but something like a tidal wave that had come charging in upon us, although it certainly was not water, and having come in, swirled and rolled with a mighty churning force.

Then it was gone and we hadn't stirred. For all the boiling and the swirling of whatever it had been, it had not affected us, for we stood, the two of us, exactly where we'd stood when we jumped up to our feet.

But the fire was gone. There was no sign of it. And instead of night, there was brilliant sunlight shining on the valley just beyond the cleft.

152

18

The valley was different. Nothing that one could pick out to start with, on the moment, and say this is not the same and something else is different. But it had a different look and as we stood in the mouth of the cleft, we began to pick out those things that were different.

There were fewer trees, for one thing, and they all were smaller. And it wasn't autumn, for all the trees were green. The grass seemed different, too, not as lush, not as green, but with a yellow cast to it.

"They did it," Cynthia whispered. "They did it without even asking us."

I stood there, wondering if this was all a fantasy that was a piece with the fantasy of O'Gillicuddy and hoping that it was, knowing that if one of them were fantasy the other surely must be.

"But he said a fraction of a second," Cynthia said, "and that would have been enough. Any little sliver of time that would shield us from the present. The flicker of an eyelash would have put us out of it."

"They blundered," I told her. "They blundered very badly."

For I knew it was no fantasy. We had been moved in time and over a much greater segment of time than the small part of a second of which O'Gillicuddy had spoken.

"They never tried it before," I said. "They weren't even sure they could really do it. We were their first experiment and the damn fools blundered."

We walked out into the valley, into the bright sunlight, and I glanced up at the cliff walls and there were no cedars growing there.

A surge of anger swept over me. There was no telling how far back we had been thrown. Back at least to a time before the cedars had taken root, and the cedar, if I remembered rightly, took an enormous amount of time to grow. Some of the cedars that had been growing on those rocky walls might have been centuries old.

We'd had it now, I thought. Before, up in our present, we had been lost in space, but now we were lost in time. And there was no way we could be sure of getting back. A time-trap, O'Gillicuddy had said, but if he knew no more of time-traps than he did of moving people into time, there could be no assurance that he could do what he said he would.

"We're a long way back, aren't we?" asked Cynthia.

"You're damned right we are," I said. "God knows how far back. And I don't suppose our clever ghosts know about it, either."

"But the ghouls were out there, Fletch."

"Of course they were," I said, "and it would have taken all of three seconds for Wolf to scatter them. There was no real need to send us back. O'Gillicuddy got stampeded."

"Wolf's not with us," said Cynthia. "Poor Wolf. They couldn't send him back. What'll we do now for a rabbit-catcher?"

"We'll catch them ourselves," I said.

"I feel lonely without Wolf," she said. "It took so little time to get used to him."

"They couldn't do a thing about it," I told her. "He was nothing but a robot . . ."

"A mutant robot," she said.

"There are no mutant robots."

"I think there are," she said. "Or could be. Wolf changed. What was it made him change?"

"Elmer threw the fear of God in him when he busted up

154

his pals. Wolf got converted quick and switched to the winning side."

"No, it couldn't have been that. Sure, it would have scared him, but it would not have changed him the way that he was changed. You know what I think, Fletch?"

"I have no idea."

"He evolved," she said. "A robot could evolve."

"Perhaps," I said, not at all convinced, but I had to say something to stop her chattering. "Let's look around a bit to find out where we are."

"And when we are?"

"That, too," I said. "If we can manage it."

We went down the valley, moving slowly and somewhat uncertainly. There was, of course, no need to hurry now; there was no one at our heels. But it was not only that. There was, I think, in our slowness and uncertainty, a kind of reluctance to travel out into this world, a fear of what it might contain, not knowing what one might expect, and a consciousness, as well, that we were in the past, in an unknown alien time and that we had no right to be there. Somehow this world had a different texture to it—not only the lack of lush greenness in the grass or the smaller trees—but a sense of some strange difference that probably had no physical basis, but was entirely psychological.

We went on down the valley, not really going anywhere, going without purpose. The hills fell back a little and the valley widened and ahead of us other hills ranged blue into the sky. We could see that the valley we were traveling joined another valley and in a mile or so we reached the river into which the stream we had been following poured its waters. It was a wide river, running very fast, its waters dark and oily with their speed and as it ran it talked in a growling undertone. It was somehow a little frightening to look upon that river.

"There's something over there," said Cynthia.

I looked where she was pointing.

"It looks like a house," she said.

155

"I don't see a house."

"I just saw the roof. Or what looked like a roof. It's hidden in the trees."

"Let us go," I said.

We reached the field before we really saw the house. A thin, scraggly stand of corn, knee-high or less, grew in uneven rows that were choked with weeds. There was no fence. The field stood on a small bench above the river and was hemmed in by trees. Here and there the rows were broken by standing stumps. Off to one side of the field bare skeletons of trees were piled in ragged clumps. Someone, not too long ago, had cleared a patch to make a field, hauling off the trees once they had been cut down.

The house stood across the field, on an elevation slightly higher than the patch of corn. It was a ramshackle affair even from a distance; it became more ramshackle as we approached it. A weedy garden lay off to one side of it and behind it was another structure I took to be a barn. No livestock was in sight. In fact, nothing living was in sight. The place had a vacant feel about it, as if someone had been there just a while ago, but now was gone. A sagging bench stood in front of the house, beside the open door, and beside it was a chair, with the legs cut down, the back ones shorter than the front so that anyone who sat in it would be tilted back. In the yard, a battered pail lay on its side, rolling a little in the wind. A sawed-off section of a large tree bole sat on its end, apparently a chopping block, for its upper end was scarred in places where an axe had struck. A cross-cut saw rested on two pegs or nails on the cabin wall. A hoe leaned against the wall.

The smell struck us when we came up to the chopping block—a sweetish, terrible smell that hit us with a slight shifting of the wind, or perhaps only the swirling of an air current that carried it to us. We backed away and the odor lessened and then, as suddenly as it had come, was gone, although it seemed that some of it still stuck to us, that we had been contaminated by it.

156

"In the house," said Cynthia. "There is something in there."

I nodded. I had the horrible feeling that I knew exactly what it was.

"You stay here," I said.

For once she didn't argue with me. She was quite content to stay there.

There was no air current this time and I got almost to the door before it came at me again. As I moved forward, it came rolling out at me, overpowering in its fetidness. I cupped a hand over my mouth and nose and went through the door.

The interior was dark and I paused for a moment, gagging, fighting down the urge to vomit. My knees were wobbly and all strength seemed to have been drained from me by the stench. But I hung in there—I had to know. I thought I knew, but I must be sure, and I told myself that the poor creature who lay somewhere in that darkened room had the right to expect that a fellow human would not turn away from him even under conditions such as these.

My eyes became more accustomed to the darkness. There was a fireplace, crudely made of native stone; a makeshift, drunken table stood to one side of it with two pans and a skillet standing on it. A chair was tipped over in the center of the room, a heap of junk lay piled in a corner, the dark shape of clothing hung from a wall. And there was a bed.

There was something on the bed.

I drove myself forward until I could see what lay upon the bed. It was black and swollen and out of the blackness two eyeballs glared back at me. But there was something wrong about it all, something terrifying, more terrifying than the dreadful stench, more frightful than the black and swollen flesh.

Two heads, not one, lay upon the pillow.

I drove myself again. Leaning over the thing upon the

157

bed, making sure that I really saw what I thought I saw, establishing beyond doubt that both the heads belonged to the single body, shared the single neck.

Then I reeled away, half-blinded. Now I doubled up and vomited.

Still retching, I staggered toward the door, but out of the corner of my eye, I saw the drunken table, with the two pans and the skillet standing on it, and I lurched at them. I got a grip on all three and, bumping against the table, knocked it over. Then I went reeling out the door, with two pans clutched in one hand, the skillet in the other.

I made it across the yard and suddenly my knees gave way and I sat down hard upon the ground. I put up a hand and wiped my face and it still felt dirty. All of me felt dirty.

"Where'd you get the pans?" Cynthia asked. What a crazy thing to ask. Where did she think I'd gotten them?

"Is there a place to wash them?" I asked. "A pump or anything."

"There's a little stream down by the garden. Maybe there's a spring."

I stayed sitting. I used a hand to wipe my chin and there was vomit on it when it came away. I wiped it on the grass.

"Fletch?"

"Yes."

"Is there a dead man in there?"

"Days dead. A long time dead," I said.

"What are we going to do?"

"What do you mean—what are we going to do?"

"Shouldn't we bury him or something?"

I shook my head. "Not here. Not now. What difference does it make? He'd not expect us to."

"What happened to him? Could you tell what happened?"

"Not a chance," I said.

She stood looking at me as I got unsteadily to my feet.

"Let's go and wash the pans," I said. "And I'd like to wash my face. Then let's pick some vegetables out of that garden . . ."

158

"There's something wrong," she said. "More wrong than just a dead man."

"You said back there," I told her, "that we should find out when we were. I think I have just found out."

"You mean the man?"

"He was a monster," I said. "A mutation. A man who had two heads, a two-headed man."

"But I don't see . . ."

"It means we are thousands of years back. We should have suspected it. Fewer trees. The yellow color of the grass. The Earth is only now groping back from war. A mutant such as a two-headed man would have no survival value. There may have been many such people in the years following the war. Physical mutants. A thousand years or so and they'd all be gone. And yet there's one lying in that house."

"You must be mistaken, Fletch."

"I hope I am," I said. "I'm fairly sure I'm not."

I don't know if I just happened to look up at the looming hillside or if some flicker of motion had alerted me, but when I looked, high up I caught a glimpse of something running, not running, really, for you could not see its feet, but something floating rapidly along, a cone-shaped thing that was moving very fast. I saw it for an instant only, then it was gone from sight. But I couldn't be mistaken. I knew I simply couldn't be.

"Did you see it, Cynthia?"

"No," she said, "I didn't. There was nothing there."

"It was the census-taker."

"It couldn't be," she said. "Not if we're as far back as you say we are. Unless . . ."

"That is it," I said. "Unless."

"You're thinking what I'm thinking?"

"I wouldn't be surprised. The census-taker could be your immortal man."

"But the manuscript said the Ohio."

"It know it did. But look at it this way: Your ancestor was an old, old man when he wrote the letter. He relied on memory and memory is a tricky thing. Somewhere he had heard about the Ohio. Maybe the old man who told him the story might have mentioned it, not as the river where the incident had happened, but as a river in the area. Through the years it would have been simple for him to come to think the story had happened on the Ohio."

She sucked in her breath, excited. "It fits," she said. "All of it. There is the river and there are hills. This could be the place."

"If it weren't the Ohio," I said, "if he was mistaken about the Ohio, it could be any one of a thousand places. A river and some hills. That's not much to go on, is it?"

"But he said the man was a man."

"He said that he looked like a man, but he knew he was no man. Something strange about him, something unhuman. That was when he first saw him. The thing he first thought was not a man could later have appeared to him very much a man."

"You think this could be it?"

"I suppose I do," I said.

"If it was the census-taker, why should he run from us? He would know us—no, that's wrong. Of course he wouldn't know us. He hasn't met us yet. It will be centuries yet. Do you think that we can find him?"

"We can try," I said.

We went plunging up the hillside. We forgot about the pans. We forgot about the garden and the vegetables. I forgot about the vomit on my chin. The way was steep and rough. There were trees and clumps of tangled bushes. There were great ledges of rock we could not climb, but had to skirt. In places we clawed our way, hanging onto trees or brush to pull ourselves ahead. There were times when we went on hands and knees.

As I climbed I asked myself, far in the back of my mind, why there should be so much urgency in the situation as to send us clawing madly up the hill. For if the house of the immortal man was somewhere on the hilltop, we could take our time and it still would be there when we reached the

160

crest. And if it were not, then there was no sense in it at all. If it were only the census-taker that we sought, he could even now be well-hidden or very far away.

But we kept on climbing up that tortuous slope of ground and finally the trees and brush thinned out and ahead of us we saw the bald top of the hill and the house that sat on top of it—a weather-beaten house with the weight and sense of years upon it, but in no way the sort of house in which I'd found the dead man. A neat picket fence, newly painted white, ran across its front and all around it, and there was a flowering tree, a blaze of pink, beside the door and roses that ran along the fence.

We flopped down on the ground and lay there, panting. The race was won and the house was there.

Finally we sat up and looked at one another. Cynthia said, "You're a sight. Let me clean you up." She took a handkerchief out of her jacket pocket and scrubbed my face.

"Thanks," I said when she was through. We got to our feet and walking side by side, sedately, as if we might have been invited guests, we went up to the house.

As we went through the gate we saw that a man was waiting for us at the door.

"I had feared," he said, "that you might have changed your mind, that you weren't coming."

Cynthia said, "We are truly sorry. We were somewhat delayed."

"It's perfectly all right," said the man. "Lunch just reached the table."

He was a tall man, slender, dressed in dark slacks and a lighter jacket. He wore a white shirt, open at the throat. His face was deeply tanned, his hair was wavy white, and he wore a grizzled moustache, neat and closely clipped.

We went into the house, the three of us. The place was small, but furnished with a graciousness that would not have been expected. A sideboard stood against one wall and upon it sat a jug. A table stood in the center of the room, covered with a white cloth and set with silver and

161

sparkling crystal. There were three places. There were paintings on the wall and a deep-pile carpet on the floor.

"Miss Lansing, please," said our host, "if you will sit here. And Mr. Carson opposite you. Now we can begin. The soup's still hot, I'm sure."

There was no one else. There were just the three of us. And surely, I thought, someone other than our host must have prepared the luncheon, although there was no evidence of anyone who had, nor of a kitchen, either. But the thought was a fleeting one that passed away almost as soon as it had occurred, for it was the kind of thought that did not fit in with this room or with the tables.

The soup was excellent, the salad crisp and green, the chops were done to a perfect turn. The wine was a pure delight.

"It may interest you to know," said our gracious host, "that I have given some very close thought to the possibilities of the suggestion you made, not entirely flippantly, I hope, the last time that we met. I find it a most intriguing and amusing thing that it might be possible to package the experiences, not only of one's self, but of other people. Think of the hoard we might then lay up against our later, lonely years when all old friends are gone and the opportunity for new experiences had withered. All we need to do then is to reach up to a shelf and take down a package that we have bottled or preserved or whatever the phrase might be, say from a hundred years ago, and uncorking it, enjoy the same experience again, as sharp and fresh as the first time it had happened."

I heard all this and was surprised, of course, but not as surprised as I should have been, somewhat after the fashion of a man who dreams a fantasy and knows even as he dreams it that it is a fantasy, but one that seems beyond his power to do anything about.

"I have tried to imagine," said our host, "the various ingredients one might wish to compound in such a package. Beside the bare experience itself, the context of it, one might say, he should want to capture and hold all the

162

subsidiary factors which might serve as a background for it—the sound, the feel of wind and sun, the cloud floating in the sky, the color and the scent. For such a packaging, to give the desired results, must be as perfect as one can make it. It must have all those elements which would be valuable in invoking the total recall of some event that had taken place many years before. Would you not say so, Mr. Carson?"

"Yes," I said, "I suppose I would."

"I have wondered, too," he went on, "by what criterion one should select the experiences to be packaged. Would it be wise to pick only the joyful ones or should one mix in a few that are somewhat less than joyful? Perhaps it might be well to preserve a few that carried a keen embarrassment, if for no other reason than to remind one's self to be humble."

"I think," said Cynthia, "that one should select a wide spectrum, being sure, of course, to lay in a large supply of the more satisfactory ones. If there should be no later urge to use some of the less satisfactory ones they could be safely left upon the shelf, untouched."

"Now, do you know," said our host, "that had been my thought exactly."

It was all so fine and comfortable and friendly, so very civilized. Even if it were not true, one wanted to believe it was; I found myself holding my breath, as if, by breathing, I might shatter an illusion.

"There is another thing one must take into consideration also," he said. "Given such an ability, does one remain satisfied with the harvesting of experiences in the natural course of life or does one attempt to create experiences he has reason to believe may serve him in the future?"

"I believe," I told him, "that it might be best to gather as one goes along, without making any special effort. It would seem more honest that way."

"As an auxiliary to all of this," he said, "I have found myself speculating upon a world in which no one ever grew up. I admit, of course, that it is a rather acrobatic feat of

163

thinking, not entirely consistent, to leap from the one idea to the other. In a world where one was able to package his experiences, he merely would be able to relive at some future time the experiences of the past. But in a world of the eternally young he'd have no need of such packaging. Each new day would bring the same freshness and the everlasting wonder inherent in the world of children. There would be no realization of death and no fear born of the knowledge of the future. Life would be eternal and there'd be no thought of change. One would exist in an everlasting matrix and while there would be little variation from one day to the next, one would not be aware of this and there'd be no boredom. But I think I may have dwelled upon this subject for too great a length of time. I have something here to show you. A recent acquisition."

He rose from the table and strode over to the sideboard, picking up the jug. He brought it back and handed it to Cynthia.

"It is a hydria," he said. "A water jug. Sixth-century Athenian, a fine example of the black-figure style. The potter took the red clay and tamed it a little with an admixture of the yellow and filled out the engravings with a brilliant black glaze. If you'll look down at the base of it, you'll see the potter's mark."

Cynthia twisted the jug about. "Here it is," she said.

"In translation," said our host, "it reads 'Nicosthenes made me.'"

She handed it across the table to me. It was heavier than I'd thought. Engraved upon its side, inlaid with the glaze, a stricken warrior lay, with his shield still strapped upon his arm, grasping his spear, butt upon the ground, with the blade pointed upward. Twirling the jug, another figure came into view—another warrior leaning dejectedly upon his shield, with his broken spear trailing on the ground. You could see that he was tired and beaten; fatigue and defeat were etched into every line of him.

"Athenian, you say?"

He nodded. "It was a most lucky find. A prime example

164

of the best of Greek ceramics of the period. You will notice
that the figures are stylized. The potters of those days never
thought of realistic accuracy. They were concerned with
ornament, not with form."

He took the jug from me and put it back upon the
sideboard.

"I fear," said Cynthia, "that we must leave. It is getting
late. It was a lovely lunch."

It all had been strange before, although quite comfortable, but now the strangeness deepened and reality got
foggy and I do not recall much more until we were out the
door and going through the gate of the picket fence.

Then the reality came back again and I spun around.
The house was there, but it was more weather-beaten,
more ruined than it had seemed. The door stood half open,
swinging in the gale that swept the hilltop and the ridgepole
sagged to give it a swayback look. Panes of glass were
broken from the windows. There was no picket fence or
roses, no blooming tree beside the door.

"We've been had," I said.

Cynthia gasped. "It was so real," she said.

The thing that hammered in my brain was why he,
whoever he had been, had done it. Why play so elaborate a
piece of magic? Why, when it might have served his purpose better, had he not allowed us to come upon a deserted
and time-ruined house in which it would have been apparent no one had lived for years? In such a case we'd
simply have looked it over and then gone away.

I strode up to the door, with Cynthia following, and into
the house. Basically it was the same as it had been, although no longer neat and gracious. There was no carpet
on the floor, no paintings on the wall. The table stood in
the center of the room and the chairs were there, as we had
sat in them, pushed back the way we'd left them when we'd
gotten up to leave. But the table was bare. The sideboard
stood against the wall and the jug still stood upon it.

I went across the room and picked it up. I carried it to
the door where the light was better. It was the same piece,

as far as I could see, as the one our host had shown us.

"Do you know anything of Greek ceramics?" I asked Cynthia.

"All that I know is that there was black-figure pottery and red-figure pottery. The black came first."

I rubbed a thumb across the potter's mark.

"You don't know, then, if this says what he said it did."

She shook her head. "I know potters used such marks. But I couldn't read one. There's something else about it, though. It looks too new, too recent, as if it had come out of the kiln only a little while ago. It shows no weathering or aging. Usually such pottery is found in excavations. It has been in the soil for years. This one looks as if it never had been buried."

"I don't think it ever has—been buried, I mean," I said. "The Anachronian would have picked it up at the time that it was made, or very shortly after, as a prime example of the best work being done. It has been carefully taken care of as a part of his collection through all the centuries."

"You think that's who he is?"

"Who else could he be? Who else, in this battered age, would have a piece like this?"

"But he is so many people. He is the census-taker and the distinguished man who had us to lunch and the other, different kind of man my old ancestor saw."

"I have a hunch," I said, "he can be anything at all. Or at least make one think he's anything at all. I rather suspect that, as the census-taker, he shows us his actual self."

"Then in that case," said Cynthia, "there is a treasure trove underneath our feet, deep down in the rock. All we have to do is find the entrance to the tunnel."

"Yes," I said, "and once we found it, what would we do with it? Just sit around and look at it? Pick up a piece and fondle it?"

"But now we know where it is."

"Exactly. If we can get back to our own present, if the shades know what they're doing, if there really is a time-trap, and if there is, it doesn't take us ten thousand years in-

166

to the future as measured by our natural present time . . ."

"You believe all these things you're saying?"

"Let's say this: I recognize them as possibilities."

"And, Fletch, if there is no time-trap? If we're stuck back here?"

"We'll do the best we can. We'll find a way."

We went out the door and started down the bluff. Below us lay the river and the cornfield, the house where the dead man lay, the weedy garden by the house.

"I don't think," said Cynthia, "that there will be a time-trap. The shades are no scientists; they are bunglers. A fraction of a second, they said, and then they sent us here."

I grunted at her. This was no time for talk like that. But she persisted. She put out a hand to stop me and I turned to face her.

"Fletch," she said, "there has to be an answer. If there is no time-trap."

"There may be one," I said.

"But if there's not?"

"In such a case," I said, "we'll come back to that house down there. We'll clean it out. It's a place to live, there are tools to work with. We'll save seed from the garden so we can plant other gardens. We'll fish, we'll hunt, we'll live."

"And you'll love me, Fletch?"

"Yes," I said, "I'll love you. I guess I already do."

19

We went down across the cornfield and I wondered as we went if Cynthia might be right—not because O'Gillicuddy and his band were bunglers, but because they were Cemetery. O'Gillicuddy, when I'd asked him, had carefully pointed out that Cemetery had no hold on them because there was nothing Cemetery could do against them and nothing that they wanted. On the face of it, this would seem to be quite true, but how could one be certain it was true? And what better tool could Cemetery use to get rid of us than O'Gillicuddy and his time ability? Surely if we were placed in another time and no way to get back Cemetery would be certain of no further interference.

I thought of my own pink world of Alden—Cynthia's world, as well. I thought of Thorney pacing up and down his study, talking of the long-lost Anachronians and fuming at the indiscriminate treasure-hunters who looted primitive sites and robbed archaeologists of their chance to study ancient cultures. And I thought with a bit of bitterness of my own fine plans to make a composition of the Earth. But mostly, I guess, I thought of Cynthia and the rotten deal she'd gotten. She, of all of us, had had the least to gain from this wild adventure. She had started out by serving as an errand boy for good old Thorney and see what it had got her.

If there were no time-trap, what could we do other than what I'd told her we would do? I could think of nothing else to do, but it would be a bleak life at the best. It was not the kind of life for Cynthia—nor for me. Winter would be coming soon, most likely, and if there were no time-trap, we'd have little time to get ready for it. We'd have to tough it through somehow, and when spring had come around we might have, by that time, figured out a better way.

I tried to quit thinking about it, for it hadn't happened yet and there might be no need to think of it, but try as I might I couldn't seem to get my mind away from it. The very horror of the prospect seemed to fascinate me.

We came down into the river valley and walked along the river until we came to the hollow that led to the cliff where we'd holed up after fleeing from the ghouls. Neither of us were saying anything. Neither of us, I suspect, trusted ourselves to speak.

We started up the hollow and when we turned the bend just ahead of us, we could see the cliffs and we'd be almost there. We'd not have long to wait. Fairly soon we'd know.

We rounded the bend and stopped dead in our tracks. Standing just this side of the cliffs were two war machines. There was no mistaking them. I think I would have known what they were in any case, but from having heard Elmer talk of them so often, I recognized them immediately.

They were huge. They had to be huge, to carry all the armaments they packed. A hundred feet long at least, and probably half as wide and looming twenty feet or more into the air. They stood side by side and they were most unlovely things. There was strength and ugliness in them. They were monstrous blobs. It made a man shiver just to look at them.

We stood there looking at them and they looked back at us. You could feel them look.

One of the machines spoke to us—or at least someone in their direction spoke to us. There was no way to tell which machine was speaking.

"Don't run away," it said. "Don't be frightened of us. We want to talk with you."

"We won't run," I said. There'd have been little use in running. If they wanted us, they'd have us in a minute. I was sure of that.

"No one will listen," said the machine, rather piteously.

169

"Everyone flees from us. We would be friends to the human race, for we ourselves are human."

"We'll listen to you," said Cynthia. "What have you to say?"

"Let us introduce ourselves," it said. "I am Joe and the other one is Ivan."

"I am Cynthia," said Cynthia, "and the other one is Fletcher."

"Why don't you run from us?"

"Because we're not afraid," said Cynthia. I could tell from the way she said it she was very much afraid.

"Because," I said, "there'd be no use of running."

"We are two old veterans," said Joe, "long home from the wars and most desirous of doing what we can to help rebuild a peaceful world. We have wandered very far and the few humans we have found have had no interest in what we might do for them. In fact, it seems they have a great aversion to us."

"That is understandable," I said. "You, or others like you, probably shot the hell out of them before the war came to an end."

"We shot the hell out of no one," said Joe. "We never fired a shot in anger. Neither one of us. The war was done with before we got into it."

"And how long ago was that?"

"By the best computation that we have, a little over fifteen hundred years ago."

"Are you sure of that?" I asked.

"Very sure," said Joe. "We can calculate it more closely if it means that much to you."

"It doesn't matter," I said. "Fifteen hundred is quite close enough."

And so, I told myself, O'Gillicuddy's fraction of a second had turned out to be more than eighty centuries.

"I wonder," said Cynthia, "if either one of you recall a robot by the name of Elmer . . ."

"Elmer!"

"Yes, Elmer. He said he was a supervisor of some sort on the building of the last of the war machines."

"How do you know Elmer? Can you tell me where he is?"

"We met him," I said, "in the future."

"That can't be true," said Joe. "You do not meet people in the future."

"It's a long story," I said. "We'll tell it to you sometime."

"But you must tell me now," said Joe. "Elmer is an ancient friend. He worked on me. Not on Ivan. Ivan is a Russian."

It was quite apparent there was no way to get away from them. Ivan hadn't said a word, but Joe was set to talk. Having finally found someone who would listen to him, he was not about to quit.

"There isn't any sense of you standing out there and us sitting here," said Joe. "Why don't you come aboard?"

A panel slid down in his front and a stairway came telescoping out. When the panel slid down it revealed a small, lighted room.

"It's a mechanic's berth," said Joe. "Place for the mechanics to stay and be protected if they have to work on me. Not that I suspect any of them ever did with any war machine. They never did with me, of course, but I don't think they did with many of the others, either. When something happened to us it was usually pretty bad. It took a lot to send us running for repairs. By the time we came to run there wasn't too much left. Few of us, I imagine, ever made it back to home. That was the tradition in those days. Of course we were self-repairing, to a degree at least. We could keep ourselves in operation, but we couldn't do too much when the damage got too massive.

"Well, come on aboard."

"I think it will be all right," said Cynthia.

I wasn't as sure as she was.

"Of course it will be all right," boomed Joe. "It is quite comfortable. Small, but comfortable. If you are hungry, I

171

have the capacity to mix you nourishment. Not very tasty, I suppose, but with some value as a nutrient. A quick snack for our hypothetical mechanic if he should get hungry on the job."

"No, thank you very much," said Cynthia. "We just now had lunch."

We climbed the stairs into the room. There was a table in one corner, a double-decker bunk, a couch along one wall. We sat down on the couch. The place was, as Joe had said, small, but comfortable.

"Welcome aboard," said Joe. "I am very glad to have you."

"One thing you said interests me," said Cynthia. "You said Ivan is a Russian."

"Ah, yes, indeed he is. I suppose you think that the Russian was an enemy, as he surely was. But how we came together is the story of our life. Once I had been fitted out and made ready for the war, loaded with munitions and all equipment tested, I set out across Canada and Alaska for the Bering Strait, traveling underwater for a few short miles to reach Siberia. I reported back occasionally on my progress, but not too often, for to do so might have meant detection. I had been given certain objectives, of course, and one by one I reached them, to find in every instance they had been neutralized. Shortly after I reached the first objective I could not raise the homeland and, in fact, after that, I never raised home base. I was quite cut off. At first I thought it was only a temporary failure of communications, but after a time concluded that there was something much more significant than communication failure. I wondered if my country had been finally beaten to its knees or if the few military centers might have gone even deeper underground, but whatever might be the reason for the failure, I told myself, I would carry out my duty. I was a patriot, a true-blue patriot. You understand the term?"

"I am a history student," Cynthia told him. "I understand the concept."

"So, driven by my bitter patriotism, I went on. I visited

all my assigned objectives and they all had been reduced. I did not stop there. I prowled, seeking what in those days were called targets of opportunity. I monitored the atmosphere for signals that might betray hidden bases. But there were no signals, neither ours nor theirs. There were no targets of opportunity. At times I came upon small communities of people who ran or hid from me. I did not bother them. As targets, they were too insignificant. You do not use a nuclear charge to kill a hundred people. Especially when the death of those hundred would have no possible tactical advantage. All I found were ruined cities in which still might live tiny, pitiful huddles of humanity. I found a blasted countryside, great craters, miles across, blasted to the bedrock, drifting clouds of poison, miles of once-rich land reduced to nothing—occasional clumps of dead or dying trees and not a blade of grass. There is no way to tell you how it was, no way for you to imagine how it might have been.

"So I turned homeward, going slowly, for there was no hurry now and I had much to think about. I shall not burden you with the thoughts, the sorrow, and the guilt. I was a patriot no longer. I had been cured of patriotism."

"There is one thing that puzzles me," I said. "I know there is more than one of you—human beings, that is. Perhaps several of you. Yet you speak of yourself as I."

"There was at one time," Joe said, "five of us, five men who were willing to sacrifice their bodies and their positions as human beings to man a war machine. There was a professor of mathematics, a most distinguished scholar; a military man, a general of the armies; an astronomer of considerable repute, a former stockbroker, and the last a most unlikely choice, one might think—a poet."

"And you are the poet?"

"No," said Joe. "I don't know what I am. I think I am all five of us together. We are separate minds no longer. We have become, in some strange way we cannot understand, a single mind. I am amazed at times that I, as this single mind, still can recognize myself as one or another of the five of us, but each time I have this sense of recognition it is not actually the recognition of another, but rather of myself. As if interchangeably and at different times I can be any one of us. But mostly I am not any one of us, but all of us together.

"It is the same with Ivan, although there were only four of him. But now there likewise is only one of him."

"We are leaving Ivan out of the conversation," said Cynthia.

"Not at all," said Joe. "He is a most active listener. He could speak either for himself or through me if he had the wish. Do you wish so, Ivan?"

A deeper, thicker voice said, "You tells it so well, Joe. Why don't you go ahead?"

"Well, as I was telling you," said Joe, "I was heading home, I had come to a stretch of prairie that seemed to go on forever. Steppe-land, I suppose. It was bleak and lonely and there seemed no end to it. It was there that I spotted old Ivan, here. He was far away and not much more than a speck, but when I used a telescopic optic, I knew what he was—an enemy of mine. Although, to tell the truth, by that time it was rather difficult to think in terms of enmity. Rather, I felt a thrill at just knowing that out there on the plain was something like myself. Strange identity, perhaps, but identity. Ivan told me later that he had much the same reaction, but the point was that neither one of us could know what the other thought. So we both began maneuvering and we both were rather tricky. There were a couple of times when I had Ivan in my sights and could have unloaded on him, but something held me back and I couldn't do it. Ivan, for some screwy Russian reason, has never been willing to admit that the same thing happened with regard to me, but I am sure it did. Ivan was too good a war machine for it not to happen. But, anyway, there were the two of us, sashaying back and forth, and after a day or two of this, it got ridiculous. So I said something to this effect: OK, let's break it off. We know damn well neither of

174

us wants to fight. We're probably the only two surviving war machines and the war is over and there is no longer any need of fighting, so why can't we be friends. Old Ivan, he didn't protest none, although it took a little time for him to agree to it, but finally he did. We rumbled straight toward one another, moving slow and easy, until we bumped noses. And we just sat there, nose to nose, and we stayed there, I don't know how long—maybe days or months or years. There wasn't really anything that we could do. The jobs we'd had had disappeared. There was in the entire world no longer any need of war machines. So we stayed out on that God-forsaken plain, the only living things there were for miles around, with our noses bumped together. We talked and we got to know one another so well that finally for long periods there was no need to talk.

It was good just to sit there, doing nothing, thinking nothing, saying nothing, nose to nose with Ivan. It was enough that we were together, that we were not alone. It may seem strange to say that two ungainly, ugly machines got to be friends, but you must remember that while we might be machines, we still were human beings. At that time we were not single minds. We were five minds and four minds, nine minds all together, and all of us were intelligent and well-educated men and there was a lot to talk about.

"But finally both of us began to see how footless and how pointless it was just to stay sitting there. We began to wonder if there might be people in the world that we could help. If man was going to recover from what the war had left, he would need all the help that he could get. Among the nine of us we had a lot of savvy, of a kind that man might need, and each of us was a source of power and energy if ways could be found for man to make use of that power and energy.

"Ivan said there was no use going west. Asia was finished, he said, and he'd roamed through enough of Europe to know it was finished, too. No social organization of any kind was left there. There might be scattered bands of men already sunk in savagery, but not enough of them to form any sort of economic base. So we headed east, for America, and there, in places, we found little scattered settlements—not too many, but a few—where man was slowly getting on his feet, at a point where he could use the kind of help we had to offer. But so far we have been of no help at all. The little settlements will not listen to us. They run screaming for the woods whenever we show up and no matter how we try to tell them we're only there to help they will not respond in any way at all. You two are the first humans who would talk with us."

"The trouble with that," I told him, "is that talking to us will do little good. We aren't of this time. We are from the future."

"I remember now," said Joe. "You said that you knew Elmer from the future. Where is Elmer now?"

"As of right now, he is somewhere among the stars."

"The stars? How could old Elmer . . ."

"Listen to me," I said. "Let me try to tell you. Once it became apparent what was about to happen to the Earth, a lot of people went out to the stars. One shipload of them would colonize one planet and another shipload another. After some ten thousand years of this, there are an awful lot of humans living on an awful lot of planets. The people who were recruited for the star-trips were the educated, the skilled, the technological people, the kind of people who would be needed to establish a colony in space. What were left were the uneducated, the untrained, the unskilled. That is why, even in this time, the settlements you have been trying to help need the help so badly. That probably is why they refuse your help. What is left is the equivalent of the peasants, the ne'er-do-wells . . ."

"But old Elmer, he wasn't really people . . ."

"He was a good mechanic. A new colony would need folks like him. So he went along."

"This matter of Elmer in the future and of people fleeing into space," said Joe, "is a most intriguing thing. But how come you are here? You said that you would tell us. Why don't you just settle back and tell us now?"

It was just like old-home week. It was all so good and friendly. Joe was a nice guy and Ivan wasn't bad. For the first time since we had hit the planet, it was really nice.

So we settled back and between the two of us, first me, then Cynthia, and then me again, we told our story to them.

"This Cemetery business still must be in the future," said Joe. "There is no sign of Cemetery yet."

"It will come," I said. "I wish I could recall the date when it was started. Perhaps I never knew."

Cynthia shook her head. "I don't know, either."

"There's one thing I am glad to know about," said Joe. "This matter of a lubricant. It was something we were a bit concerned about. We know that in time we'll need it and we had hoped we could contact some people who would be able to supply us with it. If they could get their hands on the crude and supply it to us, we could manage to refine it to a point where it could be used. There wouldn't have to be a lot of it. But we haven't been having too much luck with people."

"You'll get it, all refined and ready, according to your specifications, from Cemetery," I told him. "But don't pay the price they ask."

"We'll pay no price," said Joe. "They sound like top-grade lice."

"They are all of that," I said. "And now we have to go."

"To keep your appointment with the future."

"That is right," I said. "And if it happens as we hope it will, it would be nice to find you there and waiting for us. Do you think you could manage that?"

"Give us the date," said Joe, so I gave him the date.

"We'll be there," he said.

As we started down the ladder, he said, "Look, if it doesn't work. If there's no time-trap there. Well, if that should happen, there's no need to go back to that shack. Horrible job, you know, cleaning it up, dead man and all of that. Why not come and live with us? It's nothing very fancy, but we'll be glad to have you. We could go south for winter and . . ."

"Thanks, we will," said Cynthia. "It would be very nice."

We went on down the ladder and started walking up the hollow. The cleft in the cliff lay just ahead and before we reached it, we turned around to look back at our friends. They had switched around so that they were facing us and we raised our hands to them, then went toward the cleft.

We were almost in the cleft when the surging wave that wasn't water hit us, and as it receded, we stood shaken and in dismay.

For we stood, not in the hollow as we remembered it, but in the Cemetery.

20

The cliff was still there, with the twisted cedars growing on its face, and the hills were there and the valley that ran between them. But it was wilderness no longer. The stream had been confined between walls of lain rock, done most tastefully, and the greensward, clipped to carpet smoothness, ran from the foot of the cliff out to the rockwork channel. Monuments stood in staggered rows and there were clumps of evergreen and yew.

I felt Cynthia close against me, but I didn't look at her. Right then I didn't want to look at her. I tried to keep my voice steady. "The shades have messed it up again," I said.

I tried to compute how long it might take for the cemetery to stretch from its boundary as we'd found it to this place and the answer had to be many centuries—perhaps as far into the future as we had been sent into the past.

"They couldn't be this bad at it," said Cynthia. "They simply couldn't be. Once maybe, but not twice in a row."

"They sold us out," I said.

"But they could have sold us out," she said, "when they sent us so far back into the past. Why should we be sold out twice? If they simply wanted to get rid of us, they could have left us where we were. In such a case, there would have been no time-trap. Fletch, it makes no sense at all."

She was right, of course. I hadn't thought of that. It did simply make no sense.

"It must be," I said, "just their slab-sidedness."

I looked around the sweep of Cemetery.

"We might have been better off," I said, "if we had

179

stayed with Joe and Ivan. We'd have had a place where we could have lived and a way to travel. We could have gone with them everywhere they went. They would have been good company. I don't know what we have here."

"I won't cry," said Cynthia. "I'll be damned if I will cry. But I feel like it."

I wanted to take her in my arms, but I didn't. If I had touched her, she would have busted out in tears.

"We could see if the census-taker's place is where it was," I said. "I don't think it will be, but we can have a look. If I know Cemetery they will have evicted him."

We walked down the hollow and the walking was easy. It was like walking on a carpet. There was no uneven ground, no boulders that we had to dodge around. There were just the monuments and the clumps of evergreen and yew.

I glanced at some of the dates on the monuments and there was no way of telling, of course, how recent they might have been, but the dates I saw were evidence that we were at least thirty centuries beyond the time we'd hoped to reach. For some reason, Cynthia paid no attention to the dates, and I didn't mention them. Although, come to think of it, perhaps she did and made no mention of them, either.

We reached the river and it seemed much the same as it had before, except that the trees that had grown along its banks were gone to give way to the monuments and landscaping that marked the Cemetery.

I was looking at the river, thinking of how, in spite of all events, some things manage to endure. The river still flowed on, tumbling down the land between the hills, and there was no one who could stay its hurry or reduce its force.

Cynthia caught my arm.

She was excited. "Fletch, isn't that where we found the census-taker's house?"

She was pointing toward the bluffs and when I looked

where she was pointing, I gasped at what I saw. Not that there was anything about it that should have made me gasp. Except, perhaps, the utter beauty of it. What took my breath away, I am sure, was how the entire scene had changed. We had seen the place (in our own time bracket) only hours before. Then it had been a wilderness—thick woods running down to the river, with the roof of the house in which the dead man lay barely showing through the trees, and with the bare, knob-like blufftops shouldering the sky. Now it was all neat and green and very civilized, and atop the bluff where had stood the little weather-beaten house where we had enjoyed lunch with a charming gentleman now stood a building that came out of a dream. It was all white stone, but with a fragile air about it that seemed to rule out the use of stone. It lay low against the blufftop and its front had three porches supported by fairy pillars that, from this distance, seemed to be pencil-thin and narrow, rainbow-flashing windows all along its length. A flight of long stairs ran down to the river.

"Do you think . . ." she asked, stopping in mid-sentence.

"Not the census-taker," I said. "He'd never build a place like that."

For the census-taker was a lurker, a hider, a scurrier. He scurried all about, trying very hard to make sure that no one saw him, and snatched from beneath their noses those little artifacts (not yet artifacts, but artifacts at some time in the future) that would tell the story of those he was hiding from.

"But it is where his house was."

"So it is," I said, at a loss for anything else that I might say.

We walked along the river, not hurrying but looking at the place atop the bluff, finally coming to the place where the stairs came down to the river, ending on the riverbank with a plaza paved with great blocks of stone, with room made here and there, for plantings of—what else?—yew and evergreen.

181

We stood side by side, like a couple of frightened children confronted by a thing of special wonder, looking up the flight of stairs to the gleaming wonder that stood atop the bluff.

"Know what this reminds me of," said Cynthia. "The stairway up to Heaven."

"How could it? You've never seen the stairway up to Heaven."

"Well, it looks the way the old ones wrote about it. Except there should be trumpets sounding."

"Do you think that you can make it without the trumpets sounding?"

"I think," she said, "it is likely that I can."

I wondered what it was that was making her so lighthearted. Myself, I was too puzzled and upset to be the least lighthearted. The entire thing was pretty, if you cared for prettiness, but I didn't like particularly the placement of the building where the census-taker's house had been. That there must be some connection between the two of them seemed a reasonable conclusion and I found myself hard put to arrive at that connection.

The stairway was a long one and rather steep and we took our time. We had the stairway to ourselves, for there was no one else about, although a short time earlier there had been three or four people standing on one of the porches of the building.

The stairs at the blufftop ended in another plaza, much larger than the one at the river's edge, and we walked across this toward the central porch. Up close, the building was even more beautiful than it had been at a distance. The stone was snowy white, the arthitectural lines were refined and delicate, and there was about the whole of it a sort of reverential aura. No lettering was sculptured anywhere to tell one what it was and I found myself wondering, in a dumb, benumbed sort of way, exactly what it was.

The porch opened into a foyer, frozen in that hushed dimness that one associates with museums or with picture galleries. A glassed-in case stood in the center of the room, with a light playing on the object standing in the case. Two guards were standing by the door that led off the foyer—or I supposed that they were guards, for they wore uniforms. Echoing from deep inside the building could be heard the muffled sound of footfalls and of voices.

We came up to the case and there, sitting in it, was that very jug that we had been shown at lunch. It had to be the same, I told myself. No other warrior could have leaned so dejectedly upon his shield, no other broken spear trail quite so defeated on the ground.

Cynthia had leaned down to stare into the case and now she rose. "The potter's mark is the same," she said. "I am sure of that."

"How can you be so sure? You can't read Greek. You said you couldn't."

"That's true, but you can make out the name. Nicosthenes. It must say Nicosthenes made me."

"He might have made a lot of them," I said. I don't know why I argued. I don't know why I fought against the almost certain knowledge that here was the very piece that had stood on the sideboard in the census-taker's house.

"I am sure he did," she said. "He must have been a famous potter. This must have been a masterpiece for the census-taker to have selected it. And no potter, once he'd made one, would duplicate a masterpiece. It probably was made for some great man of the time . . ."

"Perhaps for the census-taker."

"Yes," she said. "That's right. Perhaps for the census-taker."

I was so interested in the jug that I did not notice one of the guards had moved over toward me until he spoke.

"You, I think," he said, "must be Fletcher Carson. Is that true?"

I straightened up to face him. "Yes," I said, "I am, but how did you . . ."

"And the lady with you is Miss Lansing?"

"Yes, she is."

"I wonder if the two of you would be so kind as to come with me."

"I don't understand," I said. "Why should we go with you?"

"There is an old friend who would like to speak with you."

"That is absurd," said Cynthia. "We have no friends at all. Not here, we haven't."

"I should hate to insist," said the guard, speaking very gently.

"Perhaps it's the census-taker," Cynthia said.

I asked the guard, "A little guy with a rag-doll face and a prissy mouth?"

"No," said the guard. "Not like that at all."

He waited for us and we stepped around the display case and went along with him.

He led us down a long corridor that was lined with other display cases and tables where many items were neatly arranged and labeled, but we moved along so smartly that I had no chance to make out any of them. Some distance down the corridor, the guard stopped at a door and knocked. A voice told him to come in.

He opened the door to let us through, then closed the door behind us, not entering himself. We stood just inside the door and looked at the thing—not a man, but a thing—that sat behind a desk.

"So here you are," said the thing. "You took your time in coming. I had begun to fear that you would not come, that the plan had gone awry."

The voice came out of what seemed to be the mechanical equivalent of a human head, attached to what might be roughly described as the equivalent of a human body. A robot, but not like any robot I had ever seen—not like Elmer, not like any honest robot. A frankly mechanical contraption that made no real concession to the human form.

"You're talking nonsense," I said. "We are here. The guard brought us. Would it be too much to ask . . ."

"Not at all," said the thing behind the desk. "We knew one another long ago. I suppose you may be pardoned for not recognizing me, for I have changed considerably. You once knew me as Ramsay O'Gillicuddy."

It seemed outrageous on the face of it, of course, but there was something in that voice that almost made me think so.

"Mr. O'Gillicuddy," said Cynthia, "there is one thing you must tell me. How many metal wolves were there?"

"Why, that's an easy one," said O'Gillicuddy. "There were three of them. Elmer killed two of them and only one was left."

He motioned at chairs set before the desk. "And now that you have tested me, please sit down. We have catching up to do."

When we were seated, he said, "Well, this is very cheerful and cozy and it is wonderful that you are here. We had it all planned out and it seemed to be so foolproof, but in temporal matters one can never be entirely sure. I shudder at the thought of what would have happened if you had not arrived. And I have every right to shudder, for I know exactly what would have happened. This all would have disappeared. Although, come to think of it, that's not exactly right . . ."

"By the phrase, all this," I said, "I suppose you mean this museum. It is a museum, is it not, housing the collection of the census-taker?"

"Then you know about the census-taker?"

"You might say we guessed."

"Of course," O'Gillicuddy said, "you would have. You both are quite astute."

"Where is the census-taker now?" asked Cynthia. "We had hoped to find him here."

"Once he had seen his collections housed," said O'Gillicuddy, "this collection and the original and much larger collection recovered from its hiding place in the old Balkans area, he took off for the planet Alden to lead an expedition of archaeologists to his old home planet. Not

185

having heard from it or any of his fellows for many centuries, he is convinced that his race has disappeared, for one of the many reasons which might bring about the disappearance of a race. So far we have had no word of the expedition. We await it anxiously."

"We?"

"Myself and all the rest of my brother shades."

"You mean you're all like this?"

"Yes, of course," he said. "It was a part of the bargain that we made. But I forget you do not know about the agreement. I shall have to tell you."

We waited to be told.

"It goes this way," he said, getting down to business. "From here we'll send you back to your own present time, to that temporal moment you would have expected to arrive at if the time-trap had worked as I said it would . . ."

"But you bungled then," I said, "and you will bungle now and . . ."

He raised a metallic hand to silence me. "We never bungled," he said. "We did what we intended. We brought you here, because if we had not brought you here the plan would not have worked. If you were not here to have the plan unfolded, you'd not know what to do. But going back with the plan in mind, you can bring this all about."

"Now, wait a minute there," I protested. "You're getting this all tangled up. There is no sense . . ."

"There is an amazing lot of sense to it," he said. "It works this way. You were in the distant past and we bring you forward to this future so you can be told the plan, then you'll be sent back to your present so you can implement the plan that will make it possible for the future you now occupy to happen."

I jumped to my feet and banged the desk. "I never have heard so damn much foolishness in all my life," I shouted. "You've got time all tangled up. How can we be brought into a future that won't exist unless we are in our present to do whatever damn fool thing we have to do to make this future happen?"

186

O'Gillicuddy was somewhat smug about it. "I admit," he said, "that it may seem slightly strange. But when you think of it, you will perceive the logic of it. Now we're going to send you back in time . . ."

"Missing your mark," I said, "by several thousand years . . ."

"Not at all," said O'Gillicuddy. "We'll hit it on the nose. We no longer depend upon mere psychic ability. We now have a machine, a temporal selector, that can send you anywhere you wish, to the small part of a second. Its development was a part of the bargain that was made."

"You talk about plans," said Cynthia, "and bargains. It might help a little if you tell us what they are."

"Given half a chance," said O'Gillicuddy, "I would be charmed to do so. We will send you back to your temporal present and you will go back to Cemetery and see Maxwell Peter Bell . . ."

"And Maxwell Peter Bell will throw me out upon my ear," I said, "and maybe . . ."

"Not," said O'Gillicuddy, "if you have two war machines standing just outside, loaded for bear and ready. They'll make all the difference."

"But how can you be sure the war machines . . ."

"You asked them, didn't you, to be at a certain place at a certain time?"

"Yes, we did," I said.

"All right, then. You will see Maxwell Peter Bell and you will let him know that you can prove he is using Cemetery as a cache for smuggled artifacts and you will tell him . . ."

"But smuggling artifacts is not against the law."

"No, of course it's not. But can you imagine what will happen to Mother Earth's carefully polished image if it should be known what is being done? There would be a smell not only of dishonesty but of ghoulery about it that would take them years to wipe away, if they ever could."

"It might work," I said, somewhat reluctant to admit it.

"You will explain to him most carefully," said

O'Gillicuddy, "being sure he does not mistake your meaning or intent, that you might just possibly find it unnecessary to say anything about it if he should agree to certain actions."

O'Gillicuddy counted the actions on his fingers, one by one. "Cemetery will agree to donate to Alden University all its holdings in artifacts, being very vigilant in recovering and turning over all that they have hidden, and henceforth will desist from any dealing in them. Cemetery will provide the necessary shipping to transport the artifacts to Alden and immediately will implement the establishment of regular passenger service to Earth at a rate consistent with other travel fares throughout the galaxy, providing reasonably priced accommodations for tourists and Pilgrims who may wish to visit Earth. Cemetery will establish and maintain museums to house the collection of historic artifacts collected since mankind's beginning by a certain devoted student who is designated by the name of Ronex from the planet Abernax. Cemetery will . . ."

"That is the census-taker?" Cynthia asked.

"That is the census-taker," said O'Gillicuddy, "and now if I might proceed . . ."

"There's one thing," said Cynthia, "that still bothers me a lot. What about Wolf? Why should he first be hunting us and then . . ."

"Wolf," said O'Gillicuddy, "was not exactly a metal wolf. He was one of the census-taker's robots that had been infiltrated into Cemetery's wolf pack. The census-taker, as you must understand, was no one's fool, and he kept a hand in almost everything transpiring on the Earth. And now if I may proceed . . ."

"Please do," said Cynthia.

O'Gillicuddy went on, counting off the points on his fingers. "Cemetery is to contribute funds and all necessary resources to a research program aimed at a reliable system of temporal travel. Cemetery likewise is to contribute all necessary funds and resources to another research program aimed at discovering and developing a method by which human personalities can be transferred in their entireties to a robotic brain and once such a method is developed the first objects of such transfers shall be a group of beings known as shades now existing on the planet Earth and . . ."

"That's how you . . ." said Cynthia.

"That's how I came to be as you see me now. But to go on. Cemetery shall agree to the appointment of a galactic watchdog commission which will not only see to it that the provisions of this agreement are carried out, but which shall, in perpetuity, examine Cemetery's books and actions and make recommendations for the conducting of its business."

He came to a stop.

"And that is it?" I asked.

"That is it," he told me. "I hope we thought of everything."

"I believe you did," I told him. "Now, if Cemetery will only buy it."

"I think they already have," said O'Gillicuddy. "You are here, aren't you? And I am here and the museum's here and the temporal selector is waiting for you."

"You thought of everything," said Cynthia, with some scorn and anger. "There is one thing you forgot. What about Fletcher's composition? How could you have forgotten that? If it hadn't been for his dream of making a composition, none of this would have come about. You don't know how he worked for it and dreamed of it and . . ."

"I thought you might ask that," said O'Gillicuddy. "If you'll just step across the hall to the auditorium . . ."

"You mean you have it here!"

"Of course we have it here. Mr. Carson and Bronco did a splendid job of it. It is a masterpiece. It has lived all these years. It will live forever."

I shook my head, bewildered.

"What's the matter, Mr. Carson?" asked O'Gillicuddy. "You should be very pleased."

"Don't you see what you've done," said Cynthia, angrily, her eyes bright with tears. "Experiencing it would

189

spoil it all. How could you possibly suggest that he see and hear and feel a work he has not even done? You should not have told him. Now it will always be in the back of his mind that he must create a masterpiece. He wasn't even thinking about a masterpiece. He was just planning to do a competent piece of work and now you . . ."

I put out a hand to stop her. "It's all right," I said. "I'll know, of course. But Bronco will be there with me. He'll keep me to the mark."

"Well, in such a case," said O'Gillicuddy, rising, "there is just one more thing for you to do before you go back to your time. There are some friends waiting outside to say hello to you."

He came spidering around the table on his unhuman legs attached to his unhuman body and we followed him out the door, down the corridor, and across the foyer.

They were lined up outside the porch, the five of them, waiting there for us—the war machines, Elmer and Bronco and Wolf.

It was a little awkward. We stood on the porch, looking at them and they looked back at us.

"We'll be waiting for you when you go back," said Elmer. "We'll all be waiting for you."

"I can understand the war machines being there," said Cynthia. "We asked them to meet us, but you . . ."

"Wolf came and got us," said Bronco.

"How could he?" I asked. "You were out to get him. You'd already gotten two of his fellows and . . ."

"He play it cute," said Bronco. "He make to play with us. He romp all around us, keeping out of reach. He lay down on his back and kick his legs in air. He grin at us with teeth. We figure he want us to follow him. He make it seem important."

Wolf grinned at us—with teeth.

"It's time to go," said O'Gillicuddy. "We only wanted you to be sure they would be waiting for you."

We turned and followed him back into the building.

I said to Cynthia, "It will soon be over for you. You can

190

go back to Alden and fill Thorney in with everything that happened . . ."

"I'm not going back," she said.

"But I don't see . . ."

"You'll be going on with your composition. Would you have room for an apprentice assistant?"

"I think I would," I said.

"You remember, Fletch, what you told me when we thought we were trapped back there in time? You said that you would love me. I intend to hold you to that."

I reached out and found her hand.

I wanted to be held to it.